DON'T HURT LAURIE!

Willo Davis Roberts

DON'T HURT LAURIE!

Drawings by Ruth Sanderson

New York 1977 *Atheneum*

Library of Congress Cataloging in Publication Data
Roberts, Willo Davis.
    Don't Hurt Laurie.
    SUMMARY: Laurie is physically abused by her mother.
Can she escape? Will anyone believe her story?
[1. Child abuse—Fiction]   I. Sanderson, Ruth.
II. Title.
PZ7.R54465DO   [Fic]   76-46569
ISBN 0-689-30571-0

DON'T HURT LAURIE!

ONE

Laurie sat on the edge of the table, not looking around her because it always frightened her to see all of the emergency room equipment. She didn't know exactly why it *should*, because the people at the hospital were always very kind to her. It didn't even hurt very much when they sewed her up, as the doctor was doing now. But she didn't like hospitals, and she'd be glad when it was over with and she could go home.

And that was funny. Not funny ha-ha, but funny odd. Because it was at home that she had everything to be afraid of.

"You're a pretty good girl," the doctor said, pausing a moment to look at the black sutures he was placing carefully to close the laceration across her left palm. "About two more, and we'll be all done."

He was different from the other doctors she remembered. He was very young and he had a lot of fuzzy hair and he didn't look like he shaved; he was very tall and skinny and he wore little round glasses with wire frames.

"Next time you're cutting up vegetables for your mother, you be more careful," he told her. "Sharp knives can do a lot of damage. You're lucky you didn't sever a tendon. Now *that* would have really given you a sore hand."

Laurie said nothing. She couldn't watch the needle going into her hand, even if it wasn't painful, so she looked at the scab on her knee and remembered how she'd got that. She hadn't had to go to the hospital that time; Annabelle had put antiseptic on it and bandaged it up, and the next day when one of the kids asked what happened, Laurie'd just said she'd fallen down.

"There. All done. And you be more careful next time, you hear?" The doctor smiled, and the nurse smiled, and Annabelle smiled. Only Laurie didn't smile; she felt as if her face would crack.

"Take this out to the girl at the desk," the doctor said, and handed Annabelle the emergency room report. "Good-bye, Laurie."

Laurie couldn't bring herself to reply, and her mother nudged her sharply as they walked out into the corridor. "Can't you be polite when someone speaks to you? Honestly, Laurie, you get more like your father every day . . . sullen, uncooperative. I just don't understand you."

Still Laurie said nothing. She knew from past experience that nothing she did or said was going to help, so why bother? Annabelle wouldn't hurt her here, not in front of all these people, no matter what she did or didn't do.

The girl on duty at the desk had already taken the information off the insurance card. Now she glanced over the form Annabelle handed her and then frowned a little.

"Is something wrong?" Annabelle was a slim, small, dark-haired woman, who had trouble standing still. She shifted her weight from one foot to the other.

The girl looked at Laurie, who stood quietly with her injured hand held carefully in front of her, palm up, so that the seven stitches showed, the black thread all tied in knots.

"You've been in here rather a lot lately, haven't you, Laurie?"

Laurie sensed her mother's indrawn breath more than heard it. It was Annabelle who answered. "What do you mean by that?"

"Don't I remember you coming in several times before this?" The girl frowned more deeply, trying to remember. "You had a broken arm . . . or was it a broken collarbone? And then you were burned . . ."

Laurie stood very still, not daring to answer, letting Annabelle do it, as she always did. She was small for nearly eleven, she knew, and the shorts and halter top she wore made her look even thinner. Her fair hair was straight and long and there was really too much of it for the size of her face. Her greenish eyes were too big, too, so that she looked like one of those children in a book illustration, the ones who aren't supposed to seem real at all. She wondered what the woman thought . . . what she would think if she knew . . .

"She's a very clumsy little girl," Annabelle said, a crispness coming into her voice. "Is there anything else you need?"

"No, Mrs. Summers. I just thought . . . Laurie's had so many accidents."

"If she'd be more careful, she wouldn't have so many. Thank you." Annabelle spun around on one sandaled foot and pushed Laurie ahead of her. "Come on, we've got to get home."

They walked out of the hospital into the spring sunshine, Annabelle's heels clattering on the cement as if she were in a hurry. They didn't say anything as they crossed the parking lot and got into the car. Annabelle drove carefully, because driving made her nervous, and Laurie sat on her own side of the seat and looked out the window.

She didn't remember exactly when she'd begun to think of her mother as *Annabelle*. It was strange, but it had been a long time since Laurie had called her anything at all.

Maybe it had started when Annabelle and Jack got married, because Jack's children called her Annabelle. And Laurie didn't want to think of her as *Mother* any more. The mothers in books were warm, protective people who explained the facts of life, even if they were embarrassed about them when you asked questions. And they baked cookies and made you dresses or, if they worked, they gave you extra allowances for fixing dinner before they came home, and on Sundays they took you to the zoo.

Annabelle wasn't like that at all.

"I guess we've got a few extra minutes," Annabelle said suddenly from beside her. "Do you want to stop at the library?"

Laurie nodded, not speaking. She hated to take any favors, but if she had a ride home she could take out more books than she could carry by herself.

"I'm going to run over to the market. I'll meet you out front in twenty minutes, then. OK?"

Laurie nodded, and slipped out of the car. She felt better as soon as her mother had driven away, and she went up the broad steps and pushed open the library door.

Later the lady at the desk in the children's section glanced at her curiously when she brought her books up to be checked.

"My goodness, what happened to you?"

Laurie swallowed. She wondered what the lady would say if she replied, "My mother hit me with a butcher knife." But of course she didn't say anything like that. She knew it would only make things worse.

"I cut my hand and had to have stitches in it," she said.

"My, that's too bad." The woman took Laurie's card and began to check out the books. "We've got a new book here you might like. It's about a little girl whose parents are being divorced. The girls your age say it's very good. Would you like to take it?"

"No, thank you," Laurie said politely, averting her eyes from the cover. "I have all I can read in two weeks, I think."

That wasn't true at all. She could read twice as many books as she was taking out, without half trying. But she didn't like books about kids and their problems with divorcing parents or alcoholic fathers or extreme poverty or troubles, troubles, troubles. She had enough problems of her own, and she didn't want to think about anyone else's, even in a pretend world where you knew everything was going to turn out all right in the end.

What she liked were fun books, where it was not only all right at the end but all the way through the book. Where it got scary, maybe, but you knew it was all in fun. Where everybody had adventures and good friends and nice mothers and fathers, and there were dogs or cats or horses for pets. She'd always wanted a pet, but Annabelle didn't like animals. A few weeks ago she'd read a swell story about a girl who found a magic ring and it got everything she'd ever wanted for her. At the end it turned out she didn't really want all those things, which Laurie thought was stupid, but she'd enjoyed reading it. At night after she went to bed she imagined what things she'd want if she had a magic ring, and she was pretty sure she wouldn't decide she didn't want them after she had them.

She held her stack of books in her good arm and went down the steps to wait for Annabelle.

When they got home, she checked the mailbox in the lobby before they went upstairs, and Annabelle paused on the steps to see what she was doing.

"I took the mail up hours ago. What are you looking for?"

"Nothing," Laurie said, shifting the weight of the books to her other arm, but balancing them so they didn't touch her hand, which was beginning to ache now.

Annabelle was a pretty woman, but sometimes, when her mouth twisted the way it did now, Laurie didn't think she was attractive at all. "Nothing. That's why you're looking in the mailbox, for nothing? What are you looking for? A birthday card? From your father?" She hugged the grocery bag tighter to her chest. "Honest to God, Laurie, I should think you'd give up. He's never going to send you a birthday card, he never has, has he? Can't you get it through your head, he doesn't care about you and he never will."

Laurie followed her up the stairs silently.

"I wish you'd answer when I speak to you. It's rude not to say something when someone speaks to you," Annabelle said, but Laurie only swallowed. She couldn't think of anything to say.

It was true her father had never sent her a birthday card, but one year she'd gotten a valentine from him, the year she was nine. It had been forwarded three times, so it didn't come until the middle of March, and it was supposed to be a funny card, but it made Laurie cry. She still had it, hidden away in a box where she hoped her mother wouldn't discover it and ridicule her for saving it.

"Jack's going to be home tonight, so do a quick dusting in the living room," Annabelle said as they went into the apartment. "And don't leave your books around where he can trip over them again."

That had only happened once, six months ago, right after she and Jack were married, but Annabelle kept bringing it up. Laurie decided she didn't have to make a mistake but once, and people kept throwing it in her face for the rest of her life.

She moved silently, carrying the books into the room she shared with her stepsister, Shelly. Shelly was only four, and although she was an inoffensive little girl, Laurie hated sharing a room with her. It meant the lights had to be put out early so Shelly could go to sleep. Even a reading light bothered her, Annabelle said, although Shelly never seemed to wake up once she'd gone to sleep.

She was there now, having a make-believe tea

party with the dishes Jack had brought back from Atlanta his last trip. She looked up, a plump, smiling, blonde little girl, and drank imaginary tea.

"Would you like some tea, Laurie?"

"No, thanks." Laurie dumped her books on the bed, wishing that just once she could come home and go into a room and close the door and be all by herself.

"Daddy's coming home tonight," Shelly informed her.

"I know it." Laurie dreaded the nights when Jack came home. It wasn't that he was mean to her; certainly he'd never pushed her down the stairs or thrown boiling water on her or slashed out at her with a knife. But she knew he didn't like her, not really, and she tried to stay out of his way, just in case. She didn't try to put into words, just in case *what*.

She only faintly remembered her own father. Annabelle said he didn't care about her, that he never had and never would. Maybe that was true, because certainly he'd gone away and left them when she was only three years old; and though she'd prayed and prayed that he would come back, he never had.

She could remember a few times when he'd played with her, and she thought she recalled sitting on his lap while he read to her out of a book with brightly colored pictures in it. There was a hazy memory, too, of being with her father in a boat, out on the water, and he'd dripped water on her from the oars and then laughed when she squealed.

He had liked her once. She was sure of that. And sometimes she tried to convince herself that he hadn't come back for her simply because he hadn't been able to find her, the way they moved around all the time.

Other times she had to admit to herself that if he'd really wanted to locate them, he'd have managed it. For a long while, until her grandmother had died, *she* had known where they were. Annabelle hadn't liked her own mother very well, and she hadn't really bothered to keep in touch; but once in a while when she was sick or out of work or something she had left Laurie with Grandma Denvers for a few weeks or a month.

Laurie hadn't liked Grandma Denvers especially well, either, for she was old and sick and crabby. All she ever talked about was how sick she was, and how ungrateful Annabelle was, and how the only time they came around was when they wanted something from her. Laurie had never wanted anything from her, but she couldn't help it if her mother dumped her off there until she found another job. For a while Laurie had thought the old woman was just pretending to be sick, but she'd died so she must have really had something the matter with her.

Grandma Denvers hadn't liked Harry Kolman, either. Harry was Laurie's father. She had said the same things about him that Annabelle did, that he was a worthless, no-good skunk. She had said, too, that Laurie was the spitting image of him; and when she said that she'd looked at Laurie as if to include her in the worthless, no-good category, too.

Laurie wasn't sure what to believe about her father, but sometimes she'd pretend she'd had a letter from him, and that he said he was coming to get her and take her to live with him somewhere far away from Annabelle. Like in Mexico or California or some place like that. Once it had been so real to her that she'd almost confided in a girl at school that she wouldn't be there much longer, because she was going to live with her father.

That had been sort of frightening, realizing she'd believed something she'd made up that way, and after that she tried not to let her imagination run away with her again. And the past couple of years, since Grandma Denvers had died, they really *had* moved so often it would have taken a Pinkerton man to find them. Only she supposed there weren't any Pinkerton men anymore. Nobody, Laurie knew, was going to come along and take her away from Annabelle.

"Laurie!" Annabelle's voice was sharp, coming from the kitchen. "Can't you answer the phone? You know I'm busy!"

She hadn't even heard the bell, but she moved to obey, speaking in a quiet voice. "Summers' residence," she said, the way she'd been taught.

The voice on the other end of the line was young and uncertain. "Oh . . . I'm sorry. I thought this was the number for the Kolmans . . ."

Shirley Rogers, Laurie thought. She recognized the voice because Shirley had asked her to share a table at lunch a few times lately. "This is Laurie Kolman," she said quickly.

"Oh, hi, Laurie. I forgot . . . your mother is remarried, isn't she?"

"Yes." Laurie wanted to say something friendly, but she couldn't think what. From the kitchen Annabelle called out, "Well, who is it? What do they want?"

Laurie put her hand over the receiver and said, "It's for me," and then Shirley said, "I wanted to ask you to a party, Laurie. It's my birthday on Saturday, and my father said I could have a theater party. We'll meet at my house and my mother will take us to the show, and then we'll come back home for cake and ice cream afterward. We have to be at the show at two, so we'll get together about one thirty. Will you come?"

Annabelle had come to the doorway and was standing there frowning. "It's for you? Who is it?"

Laurie couldn't remember that anyone from school had ever called her at home before. And she'd never been to a birthday party, either; she never went to the same school long enough to get that friendly with anybody.

"I . . . think I'd like that. I'll have to ask my . . . mother, though."

"OK. You can let me know tomorrow in school. I'll see you then," Shirley said.

Laurie said good-bye and hung up, her mouth dry. Annabelle was bearing down on her, wiping her hands on a dish towel.

"What was that all about?"

"A girl named Shirley Rogers invited me to a birthday party on Saturday." Laurie said it with a mixture of hope and apprehension.

"I never heard you talk about anyone named Shirley Rogers. Why is she inviting *you*?"

"Maybe she likes me. She's asked me to eat with her and the other girls a few times."

Annabelle sniffed, heading back toward the kitchen. "More likely she's just looking for as many presents as she can get. Honestly, when she hardly knows you!"

Laurie licked her lips. "She's been friendly. And it's a theater party, they're going to take us all to the show. So that'll cost them as much as the presents will, won't it?"

Annabelle didn't answer. She was peeling potatoes at the sink. Laurie stood in the doorway, watching.

"Can I go?"

"We'll have to think about it."

"I have to give her an answer in school to-morrow."

"Well, I'll talk to Jack about it," Annabelle said, and that was the end of the conversation.

Laurie knew perfectly well that Jack wouldn't care, one way or the other. If it had been his own kids, Tim or Shelly, he'd have been amazed to have them even bother to ask if they could go. He let

Tim and Shelly do just about anything they wanted.

She dusted the living room and made sure there was a clean ashtray beside the recliner. Jack smoked a cigar every night after dinner, when he was home. They smelled awful, and when everybody knew they caused cancer, Laurie couldn't imagine why anyone would smoke them, but she set out the ashtray, anyway.

Then she straightened up the magazines and put them in the rack. Annabelle read a lot of magazines, although she was always complaining about how busy she was and how she never had any time to herself.

The radio was on in Tim's room, and Laurie stopped and looked in. She liked Tim better than she did Shelly. He was only eight, but he was pretty sharp for a little kid. He had dark hair and eyes, like Jack, but that was the only thing they had in common so far as she could see.

Tim was building a model airplane. He spoke without taking his eyes off the piece he was fitting to it. "Hi. Shelly says Dad's coming home tonight. Do you know if he'll be here over the weekend?"

"I don't know. Nobody said." Sometimes Jack was home for several days, sometimes only overnight. He sold electronics equipment, and he traveled all over the country. "That's turning out real nice, Tim."

"Yeah, isn't it? Hey." He turned and saw her hand with the black sutures in it. "What happened, Laurie?"

For a few seconds they stared at one another, wordless communication between them. Then Tim swung his head around toward the kitchen, as if he could see through the walls.

"Did *she* do it?"

Laurie hesitated, then nodded. She'd never told anyone about the things Annabelle did to her. And Annabelle never did them when there were witnesses around. But Tim was almost like her real brother, and she knew he wouldn't tell anyone, either.

Tim looked at the stitches, his brown eyes serious. "Why does she do it, Laurie? She pushed you the time you fell down the stairs, too, didn't she? You didn't just fall like she said?"

"I don't know why she does it," Laurie said slowly. "I guess she hates me because I remind her of my father. He had blond hair and green eyes and he was skinny, like me. She was really mad when he deserted us."

Tim nodded, going back to his model. "Well, she'd better not do anything to Shelly or me, or I'll tell Dad. Did you ever tell anybody what she does?"

She shook her head. There had never been anyone to tell. There probably never would be. She'd have to live with Annabelle until she was old enough to get out of school and have a job. When she was eighteen, surely. But eighteen was such a long way off.

Laurie sat down on the bed and watched Tim build his airplane and wondered how she was going to stand it for another seven years.

TWO

THE APARTMENT WAS A DIFFERENT place when Jack was there. He was a big man, and he wore bright clothes and talked in a loud voice and laughed a lot. That ought to have made him seem jolly, Laurie thought, but somehow he didn't strike her as jolly, not really.

Oh, he played with his kids, and held Shelly on his knee and made her beg for the present he'd brought her, and he laughed at whatever she told him about what she'd done while he was gone. But Laurie didn't find him either friendly or amusing.

Tonight the present was a fuzzy plush tiger. Shelly clasped it to her chest, her little round face laughing, her golden curls tumbling over her forehead. "I like it, Daddy, I like it!" she cried, and Jack swept her off her feet and tossed her into the air while she crowed with delight.

My father used to do that to me, too, Laurie thought. Where was he now? Had he truly forgotten all about her?

Jack put Shelly down and turned toward Laurie. "Well, what have you been doing, young lady?"

She hated herself because she never could think of anything to say to him, and then he thought she was hostile or sullen. She felt the warmth creeping up her neck and tried desperately for something, anything, in the way of a response. "Just . . . reading."

"Reading, eh?" His voice always changed when he spoke to her. He still made it loud and jolly, but it was as if he forced the interest rather than really felt it, the way he did with Shelly and Tim. "You are the readingest kid I ever saw. Well, I brought you something, too. I didn't buy this one, I found it on the beach."

He pulled it out of his pocket and passed it over to her, and Laurie put out her hand. It was a shell, small enough to hold comfortably in her palm. It was a pale pink and delicately shaped, as if it had been rolled up by a master craftsman.

Laurie stared at it. "It's . . . beautiful," she said softly. "Thank you." And when she looked up at him, she thought he looked pleased at her delight.

She didn't call him anything, either. She couldn't

call him *Daddy*, the way his own kids did, and to have addressed him as *Jack* was equally impossible.

And then he saw her left hand. The laughter went out of his face, and he swore. "What happened to you?"

Laurie's glance slid toward Annabelle, who was hovering in the doorway. Her mother came toward them now, wiping her hands on her apron.

"Oh, she slipped with a knife and had to have stitches. Honestly, you'd think at nearly eleven she'd know enough to be more careful, wouldn't you? Come on, everybody, dinner's ready, and we're having steak so let's not let it get cold."

Annabelle was an expert at smoothing over things like this. She always did it in the same way. She'd say how Laurie had tripped over her own feet . . . she had big feet like her father . . . or how she'd been careless in some way. And then she'd have something they had to do immediately, so nobody could ask questions.

As they walked toward the dining area, Jack rested a hand on Laurie's shoulder. It was the first time she could remember that he'd touched her; the hand was warm and heavy and made her feel peculiar, although she couldn't have said how and why.

"Well, you'd better be more careful, girl. It's going to get you out of washing dishes for a few days, though, eh?"

It probably wouldn't have, but if Jack was going to be home for a while, Annabelle wouldn't make

her wash dishes now. Annabelle seldom did anything to directly cross her new husband.

They were almost finished with dinner, and Laurie, as usual, had eaten very little, when Shelly piped up, "Laurie's going to a party, aren't you, Laurie?"

"That right?" Jack was having his coffee and groped in a pocket for his cigar. "What kind of a party, Laurie?"

He was looking right at her, waiting for an answer; otherwise she'd never have mentioned it to him.

"It's a birthday party for a girl in my class. On Saturday." She didn't look at Annabelle, who was watching her closely.

"A birthday party, eh? Well, then you'll need some money for a present, won't you?" He pulled out his wallet and peeled off a five dollar bill. "There, is that enough to get a good present?"

Annabelle opened her mouth, as if to protest either the assumption that Laurie was going to the party or the amount of money, but then she thought better of it. Laurie accepted the bill, waited a moment to see if her mother was going to demand that she give it back, and then said "Thank you" for the second time that evening.

So it was settled, and Annabelle hadn't had a chance to put it to Jack in a way that would have made him refuse to allow her to go. Laurie felt a small inner warmth as she helped clear the table.

Some of the warmth was dissipated, however, when she heard Annabelle start in on Jack as soon as they were settled before the television, half an hour later.

Annabelle wanted to move.

She was smart enough not to clobber him with it, and at first Jack sort of resisted the idea. Laurie took no hope from that; what Annabelle wanted, Annabelle would get, one way or another. She pointed out that Tim and Shelly had to cross a dangerous street to get to school from here. And that Mrs. Loeber across the hall complained if they played the TV at all after nine o'clock at night, even though they kept the volume down. And that there were constant problems with the plumbing, and the landlord wouldn't fix it so it would stay fixed.

Laurie stopped listening. It didn't matter what either of them said tonight. Sooner or later, Annabelle would get her way. She always did. None of what she was saying was the real reason she wanted to move, but Jack wouldn't know that. Only Laurie knew.

Partly it was because the girl at the hospital had recognized Laurie this time, remembered she'd been in several times before because of "accidental" injuries. Annabelle wouldn't dare take her back there again, not ever, for fear someone would investigate and see why an eleven-year-old girl should hurt herself so often.

And then there was the fact that Laurie was making friends with a few kids at school. She was shy and never sought anyone out, although she was pleased on the rare occasions when the other kids invited her to join them at anything. She was looking forward to going to Shirley's party; but she'd bet her life Annabelle would see to it they moved before she got invited to anything else.

She wasn't quite sure why she was so certain that Annabelle didn't want her to make any close friends, but she *was* sure. Everytime she'd ever got friendly enough with anyone to be invited to their home, Annabelle had managed to spoil it some way. She didn't want Laurie to go into anyone else's home, and Laurie had never dared to ask anyone to her own, either.

Jack's present for Tim had been another model, and she sat for a few minutes watching him sort out the pieces. Then she went into her room to read until she had to turn out the light for Shelly. She took the little curly pink shell, placed it on the stand beside her bed, and pretended it was a birthday present from her father, instead of from Jack. And then she felt guilty about it, because Jack had tried to find something that would please her, and he'd brought her a gift the same as he'd brought for his own kids, even if he had found it on the beach instead of buying it in a store.

When she lay awake after the lights were out, she couldn't help thinking of Harry Kolman and wondering where he was, and if he'd ever come and find her. Once in a while she had to pretend that he would, even if she knew it wasn't very likely, because if she didn't it was hard not to cry.

Her injured hand throbbed in spite of the aspirin she had taken before she went to bed, and a few tears squeezed through because of that. They weren't because she had to keep on living with Annabelle and wondering what she'd do next, Laurie told herself. Anybody was entitled to cry when they hurt, even Annabelle would admit that.

But she wasn't going to let Annabelle know she was crying. She held the edge of the sheet over her mouth and cried very, very quietly, so that not even Shelly in the next bed could hear her if she woke up. And after a while the hand didn't hurt so much and she fell asleep.

Usually she didn't mind school too much, except for when she was going to a *new* school. Or when she had an injury to explain. She had a good imagination to account for the injuries, but she always felt peculiar when she told lies. Even when she knew she *had* to lie because telling the truth would only get her into more trouble.

Today school was miserable. Laurie tried to keep her hand so that the stitches didn't show, but it ached enough so that she had a hard time concentrating on what the teachers were saying. She looked up at the clock, judging how much time there was until the end of arithmetic class, and didn't hear her name until Mrs. Leaman said crossly, "Laurie, please pay attention! Will you read problem six and give us your answer, please?"

Laurie's heart thudded and her mouth went dry, the way it always did when she had to recite. Everybody was looking at her. She kept her palm down to hide the stitches, and turned to the right page with her other hand.

"My answer is—" she began, but Mrs. Leaman interrupted.

"Read the entire problem first, Laurie. Then tell us the steps you took to solve it. *Then* give us your answer."

She wished she didn't get so rattled when the teacher called on her. The problem was right there in the book, and she'd worked it out, so why should she be so nervous? Nobody else seemed to have such a bad time over a simple arithmetic problem.

She read from the book, then explained her solution. Mrs. Leaman said, "That is correct. Michael, will you take problem seven?"

Laurie wiped a damp palm on her skirt. Maybe if she ever went to the same school long enough to get acquainted, so that she felt the other kids were her friends, reciting wouldn't be so difficult.

When the bell rang, the class trouped outside for recess. Next year there wouldn't be any such thing as recess. She'd be in classes all day except for noon hour.

Laurie followed the others into the spring sunshine. Two scuffling boys jostled her hand and set it throbbing, and she held it against her, moving out of their way.

She wouldn't care if there were no recess periods. She wasn't often asked to join in any group activities anyway, because she was a stranger. The kids were getting up a game of softball, and some of the girls were jumping rope. Laurie turned away, following the line of the fence around the grounds. If she walked briskly, she should have time to go all the way around before the bell rang again.

She didn't get around even once, for at the first corner her attention was drawn to something, a bit of dirty white up against the fence. At first she thought it was only a torn piece of paper, and then it moved and made a small sound.

A kitten!

Laurie forgot her hand and ran across the grass, stooping beside it. A young kitten, its fur bedraggled, meowed plaintively as she picked it up and cradled it against her chest.

"Poor baby, are you lost?" Lost, and hungry, too, she guessed. She could count its ribs beneath the fur, and feel the rapid heartbeat, like her own when she was frightened. Laurie lifted it against her cheek, a surge of warmth rushing through her.

She'd never had a pet—Annabelle didn't like animals—but she'd always wanted one. Once she'd stroked the head of a calf, when her grandma was still living on a farm, and she'd wanted to throw her arms around it and hug it.

Not for a moment did she consider trying to keep this little waif, but that didn't stop her loving it, even if only for a few minutes.

She had a tuna fish sandwich in her lunch. Maybe there was time to go and get it and share it with the kitten.

She turned back toward the school, stepping to one side as the same pair of boys charged toward her again in whatever silly game they were playing. Only they didn't go around her, they stopped.

The bigger one, whose name was Peter, stared at her with narrowed eyes. "What's that you've got? A wet mop?"

His companion, a rather unpleasant boy named Curtis who was always tormenting someone, stepped closer to her. "A cat. A stupid cat. Give it here; let's see what sort of a ball it makes."

Laurie tightened her grip on the small creature defensively, but she was no match for the boys. One of them jerked at her hair, and the other snatched the kitten, and a moment later the poor animal was being tossed from one to the other of them. They yelled with delight, while the helpless kitten squalled its fear.

"Hey, look at that! It's a good ball, all we need is a bat and we've got a ball game!" Curtis cried.

Laurie forgot her injured hand, she forgot they were two to her one, and that they were both bigger than she was. Fury propelled her right into the middle of them, fists and feet and knees pounding and pumping and kicking. The boys fell back, astonished, and the kitten was dropped to the ground; it went scurrying away toward the fence, escaping before anyone could catch up with it.

"You're mean and rotten and horrid," Laurie said, her face growing red. "How'd you like anyone to do that to you?"

"We didn't hurt it," Peter said uneasily, for a teacher was striding toward them across the playground.

"You might have killed it! You didn't care if you hurt it or not!" Laurie cried. "How would you feel if someone bigger threw you in the air and scared you to death?"

"We didn't scare it much," Curtis said and took off, running, before the teacher was near enough to see what was going on.

"It's only a cat," Peter told her. "It wasn't scared."

But it was, Laurie thought, still trembling. *It was scared, the same way I'm scared when Annabelle is mean to me.*

She had known she couldn't possibly keep the kitten. But she was sorry it was gone. It had felt so soft and helpless in her hands, and she'd have liked to hold it a few minutes longer. She hoped it would find its way home.

The teacher, seeing they'd separated, went back toward the school.

Laurie didn't feel like walking any more. She

went to sit on a bench in the sunshine and hoped her hand would stop hurting soon.

In art class Mr. Doane announced that they were going to begin a new project; they were going to make murals to decorate the halls for Parents' Night next month.

"We will divide into teams," he said, "and each of you will be responsible for one section of the mural. I'll appoint six people to head the teams, and each of those leaders will choose a crew to work with. I know you will turn out a fine mural, one our school will be proud of."

Laurie, who had perked up at the prospect of working on a mural, sank back into her seat. She wasn't much good at team efforts; and besides, nobody would choose her. She'd had plenty of experience at being the only one left when everyone else had been chosen, because no one knew her very well. It was always humiliating when the teacher finally assigned her to a group that didn't really want her.

Today, however, it was different. One of the team leaders was Shirley Rogers, who immediately turned and said, "I choose Laurie."

Not the last one, but the first to be chosen! Laurie flushed with pleasure and moved to stand behind Shirley. The others Shirley picked were all girls, and one of them smiled at her. "I saw what you did when those nasty boys were hurting the kitten today. I thought you were very brave."

Brave? Me? Laurie thought, astonished. "I was afraid they'd hurt it," she said, and the other girl nodded.

"That Curtis is mean to animals all the time. And littler kids, too. I don't like him."

"Nobody likes him," Shirley said, having assembled her entire team. "I saw the maps you made for geography, Laurie. They were really neat. I think you're going to help us make a good mural."

"I hope so," Laurie said, and the warmth inside her was strange and good. She thought this must be what it was like when you got to be friends with other kids.

She didn't have to play baseball during P.E. class because of her hand. Laurie hated baseball, mostly because she was no good at it. Maybe if she'd ever lived in one place long enough to play in the neighborhood games with the kids, she'd have learned to hit or catch or throw. As it was, she couldn't do any of them. Just thinking about that ball coming at her was enough to make her wince. She'd been hit on the nose with a baseball once, and it had been an hour before they could stop the bleeding.

She was sitting in the bleachers watching the others when a boy wandered over and sat down one step below her. He wasn't in her class; he was much too tall and was obviously older. He looked with interest at the sutures in her hand.

"What happened to you?"

"I got cut with a knife," Laurie said. She turned her hand so that the sutures didn't show.

The boy was wearing a dirty T-shirt that said *Don't mess with me* on it in blue letters. He was quite tanned and on one bare arm there was a long thin scar, which he displayed for her.

"I had a big cut once, took eleven stitches. How many did yours take?"

"Seven," Laurie said, trying to put down the lump that rose in her throat.

"How'd you do it?" he wanted to know.

The lie came to her lips without her having to think about it. "I was cutting vegetables and the knife slipped."

"What were you doing, holding a carrot in your hand and cutting through it? Sounds kind of dumb."

Laurie said nothing. It would have been dumb, had it really happened that way. She hoped if she didn't say anything the boy would go away. She wanted friends, but not friends like this. He was only morbidly curious, the way people are about gruesome things.

"You know how I got this?" A finger traced the scar on his arm.

Laurie didn't try to answer.

"My old man threw a bottle at me. It didn't hit when he threw it, but it smashed on the stove and a chunk of it just plowed a furrow right down my arm. My old man's real mean when he's drinking. Your old man ever do things like that?"

It was as if the words were forced from her. "My father went away when I was little. I haven't seen him in years." Her heart had begun to hammer in her chest. Did he *know*?

But he couldn't know anything. Even if he guessed, if she didn't admit it, he couldn't *know*. She didn't really understand why she felt it must be a secret that her mother mistreated her; but she did know she was ashamed of it, as if in some way it were her fault.

"You're lucky," the boy said. He turned toward her, bringing up one knee and putting a foot on the seat. His sneakers were coming apart at the seams, and the laces had been mended with ugly knots. "My old man won't ever go away. He's there every night, drinkin' beer. After a few bottles he starts getting mean, and he hits everybody, throws things, swears at us all. Once he whipped me so bad they had to take me to the hospital. You ever been in a hospital?"

Out on the field the teams were changing sides. Laurie suddenly wished she were playing. She didn't want to sit here and listen to this boy talk, and yet she felt powerless to get up and walk away from him. She wondered why he wasn't playing with his own class, but she didn't ask.

"Have you?" he persisted.

"In the emergency room," Laurie said unwillingly.

"Yeah. That's where I was, in the emergency room. The old man told them I fell off a roof, but they didn't believe him. Like, I was really beat up, you know? They sent somebody out to the house to investigate, and I hoped they'd take me away and put me in a foster home, but nothing happened. I even reported him myself one time, and they asked me some questions, but nobody believed he'd really do things like that to me. When he's sober, he can talk real nice, so it was like they thought I was a liar. It don't do no good to tell anybody. They always believe your old man."

Was that why she'd never told anyone about Annabelle? Was she afraid nobody would believe her, and then it would make things worse? Because Annabelle would be very angry, if she told. Annabelle had never actually threatened her, never said what she'd do if Laurie told. She just acted as if Laurie really *had* hurt herself, as if she believed the things she told the doctors and the nurses and Laurie's teachers. But Laurie knew her mother would be furious if Laurie told anyone, and probably it was the way this boy said . . . no one would believe her, anyway.

She was glad when the P.E. class was over and she could walk away from the boy. She didn't feel sorry for him, especially; she was more angry with him, that he'd inflicted his pain on her, along with her own. There had always been the thought, somewhere in the back of her mind, that *someday* there would be someone she could talk to, someone (her father?) who would take her away.

And now this unknown boy had told her it was no use, that it would never happen.

She didn't want to believe that.

She walked home from school with Shirley Rogers and two other girls. It was the first time they'd asked her, and although she didn't say much, she enjoyed the company. They talked about the coming birthday party, but Laurie didn't tell them she was going to be eleven on Sunday.

Annabelle met her in the lobby. She was dressed in a light green spring suit, and she'd just had her hair done. She looked after the other girls.

"Who are they?"

Laurie told her. Annabelle didn't say any more, but Laurie knew she wasn't supposed to get friendly with other kids. If she got too friendly, she might have to explain some of her "accidents."

"Jack and I are going out for dinner, so Nell's coming over to stay with you kids. Let her in when she comes. I'll be back in about an hour," Annabelle said, and she was on her way.

Nell was Jack's mother, Tim and Shelly's grandmother. Laurie didn't call *her* anything, either, because she didn't know what to call her and nobody made any suggestions.

She'd only met Nell a few times, and was as wary of her as she was of most adults. Nell had never done anything to make Laurie think she was mean, but you never knew.

Nell didn't bring presents when she came. She thought Jack was foolish, and she said so, to bring a present every time he came home from a trip.

"They're only little things," Jack protested when she said that.

"But you're teaching them to expect a gift every time you come home, and that's a bad idea," Nell said. "Presents should be special, not something to take for granted."

It hadn't made any difference. Jack still brought presents. Nell actually brought presents, too, although she didn't call them that. She brought a big basket of fruit when she came that night, and it was for everybody. She put it on the dining table and said they could each have one before supper, which was going to be eaten on TV trays in the living room.

Nell was sort of plump and about the same age as Grandma Denvers had been, but she had a nice, smiley kind of face and she never talked about her aches and pains except that she'd slip her shoes off when she sat down and sort of sigh with relief, as if that felt better. She liked pretty colors; today she was wearing a soft pink dress with a pearl necklace. She didn't fuss when Shelly climbed into her lap and mussed up the dress. Once when Annabelle had scolded Shelly about this, Nell had replied, "Kids are more important than clothes." But Laurie knew Annabelle didn't agree with that. She, Laurie, didn't remember ever sitting on Annabelle's lap, even when she was very small.

One nice thing about having Nell come was that she entertained her grandchildren in the living room, and Laurie had the bedroom to herself. She made a sandwich, chose the largest of the bananas from the basket, and curled up on her bed with one of the library books.

Nell eventually noticed the stitches in her hand, of course. She didn't come right out the way everyone else had and ask how it had happened, but Laurie heard her ask Tim, later on in the evening, when they didn't know Laurie was listening.

She held her breath, but Tim only shrugged. "I don't know exactly. In the kitchen, somehow." Nell said no more, but Laurie thought the woman looked at her rather intently for a time after that.

"Annabelle says Laurie is clumsy," Shelly piped.

Nell made a snorting sound. "She doesn't seem clumsy to me," was all she said, though.

They had a quiet, pleasant evening. Laurie read almost the entire time; and since it was Friday, Shelly didn't have to go to bed early. When she did, Nell didn't say anything about turning off the light, and Shelly went to sleep at once, so Laurie was still reading when Jack and Annabelle came home.

She quickly turned out her lamp so the room was dark, but that didn't stop her from listening. She could hear what they said as Nell prepared to go.

"That's a nasty looking cut Laurie has," Nell observed. "How did it happen?"

"Oh, honestly." Annabelle laughed a little. "I don't know what I'm going to do with that child.

She is so *careless*. But I can't let her grow up without learning how to handle a knife, can I?"

"She's an odd kid," Jack commented. His voice was muffled and Laurie thought he was probably hanging something in the front closet. Then it became clear again. "Never does anything but read, never speaks unless you speak to her first, never wants to go out and do anything with the other kids. Tim really likes her, though. He says she's smart, so I guess she is."

Annabelle made a protesting sound. "Well, now, really! Of course she's smart. She gets very good report cards. And she's shy. It's hard to be shy when you're a girl."

"It isn't any harder than it would be for a boy," Jack said.

"How would you know? You were certainly never shy."

They all laughed, and Laurie heard them moving out to the hall with Nell.

When they came back in they went into their own room, and while she could hear the murmur of voices, Laurie couldn't make out their words. Annabelle had spoken of her as any mother might, she thought. As if she were proud of Laurie, as if she cared about her.

And yet there was no telling what she'd do tomorrow. No telling at all. Not for the first time she wondered what had made Annabelle the way she was. And as always before, she couldn't come up with an answer to that.

THREE

LAURIE LOOKED FORWARD WITH both uncertainty and anticipation to the party. There were ten girls invited, and all of them except Laurie had been to one another's birthday parties before.

She wore her newest dress, and saw as soon as she walked into the front room that it was too fancy for the party. Too dressy. Some of the girls were even wearing pants instead of dresses; it made Laurie feel uncomfortable, because one of her teachers had said that it was better to be underdressed than over-dressed. She wished she'd thought to ask the other girls what they were going to wear.

She could tell that the others had all been in the

Rogers' home before; they knew where Shirley's bedroom was, and the bathroom, and Mrs. Rogers called them all by name.

At first Laurie felt stiff and shy, but Shirley really made her feel at home. "Mother, this is Laurie. She's the one who drew such beautiful trees in our mural. I think we're going to have one of the best sections. Is there anybody here you don't know, Laurie?"

She almost managed to forget about her dress when some of the other girls spoke to her. Two of them had seen her protect the kitten and came to tell her they were glad. A girl who lived next door to Curtis made a face. "He's awful! Once he tried to squash a frog in our garden, and my father told him to go home and stay home! And he hit my little brother with a rock, too, and cut his head. You can be glad you don't live near him!"

Laurie nodded and smiled. Then Shirley clapped her hands for attention.

"We're not going to play any silly games," she said. "None of that baby stuff like dropping clothespins into milk cartons. We'll go to the show as soon as my dad gets here with the car. He's at the car wash with it now. It's a bus, so we can all squeeze into it at once."

They all laughed and joked about sitting on each other's laps, and Mr. Rogers when he came was good-natured and said he was glad he didn't have ten daughters all the time, all that giggling would drive him crazy. But he didn't say it the way Annabelle talked about being driven crazy, not as if he meant it.

This is what it would be like, Laurie thought, to live in the same place and know the same kids all your life. Fun. Kids to have fun with, someone to talk to, someone to confide in. Although she didn't suppose, no matter how good a friend a girl was, that she'd ever tell her about Annabelle.

The movie was about a pair of bear cubs who did comical things, and though it was really for younger kids they all laughed and enjoyed it. For once Laurie felt as if she were part of a group.

After the show they went back to Shirley's house and had chocolate cake and chocolate and strawberry ice cream, and Shirley opened her presents. She got a lot of nice things. Laurie had been uncertain about her own gift, since she didn't know Shirley very well. She remembered seeing her in the library once or twice, though, so she'd bought a pair of bookends she found on sale. One section of them was the head of a red and yellow striped bookworm, the other was his tail.

Laurie was afraid, from the fact that there were no books in the living room of the Rogers' home, that the bookends had been a mistake, but Shirley seemed delighted with them.

"I've got the whole set of the *Little House* books," she said, smiling. "I'll put them on top of my dresser with these. Thank you, Laurie."

Afterward, Laurie walked part of the way home

with a girl by the name of Jerri, whom she hadn't known before.

"I'm having a birthday in July," Jerri said. "Maybe you can come to my party, too, if my mother will let me have one this year. Last year I had a swimming party that was a lot of fun."

"I'd like that," Laurie said; it was just great to think that for once she was making friends.

But when she got home her hopeful little balloon burst as soon as she saw Tim. He was on the sidewalk outside the apartment house, squatting down poking at a stream of ants with a stick.

He looked up at Laurie and said flatly, "We're going to move."

"We are?" Not here to be invited to a party in July, not here to do the things those girls would be doing during the summer, the things she was sure they would have asked her to do, too.

"Annabelle says this place isn't a good one for kids. No yard, and we have to cross a busy street." He made a derisive sound and scraped a pile of sand into an obstruction for the ants. "As if I wasn't big enough to cross a street, for pete's sake."

It wasn't the street, or the lack of a yard, Laurie knew. It was because of *her*, because the lady at the hospital had remembered her.

"When?"

"Right away, I guess. They're out looking at places right now, before Dad goes away again. I don't think he really wants to move, but he can't stand dis-cord, either. That's what Gram says. He'd rather give in than have dis-cord in the house. Me, when I grow up, I'm going to try to be reasonable, but I'm not going to give in to any girl every time she wants something I don't want."

"All girls aren't like Annabelle," Laurie said. Disappointment made her throat ache.

Tim shot her a knowing glance. "You're not. You'll never be like Annabelle." And then, brightening, "How was the party?"

So she told him all about it, and she knew he was glad she'd had a good time. It was kind of nice, having a brother to tell things to.

They knew as soon as Jack and Annabelle came home that they'd found a place. Annabelle looked pleased and happy, and Jack was more resigned, not angry, but obviously feeling it was all a lot of fuss and work for nothing.

Getting Jack to agree to move made Annabelle very easy to live with. She fixed their favorite foods and baked Laurie a birthday cake, chocolate with pink frosting, and everybody gave Laurie presents, just like a real party except that it was all family.

Annabelle gave her blue shorts and a white shirt to go with them. (Annabelle usually gave people clothes for presents; she said they were practical.) Shelly gave her a little gold locket on a chain. Tim gave her a model he'd built, all in secret when she wasn't around. Not one of his airplanes, but a ship, a tiny replica of the *Mayflower* that had brought the

Pilgrims to America hundreds of years ago.

But it was Jack's present that really delighted her. It was in an enormous box, and he wouldn't let her pick it up. He said to open it right where it was, on the floor, because it was heavy.

It was wrapped in pink paper with a silver bow, and while she opened it, Laurie pretended to herself that this was a real party, with invited guests and favors, like the one Shirley had had.

The gift inside the box was a *Webster's Unabridged Dictionary*. She had been wanting one almost ever since she had learned to read.

The smile of anticipation slid right off her face as she sucked in a small, choked breath. "Oh, it's beautiful! It's wonderful!" she said.

"*Unabridged* means they didn't leave out half the words, like in the old one you've got," Tim informed her. Shelly looked into the box in puzzlement. "I think that's a dumb present."

Jack laughed and helped Laurie get the big book out of the box. "I thought maybe it was, too, but I cheated, Laurie. I asked Tim what to get you, and he said you'd like a good dictionary. Was he right?"

Laurie smiled at Tim, who was obviously proud of himself. "Yes, he was right."

Annabelle was clearly as surprised as Laurie at this gift. She shook her head. "Harry was always wild about books, too. I suppose that's where she gets it. Sometimes she's so much like her father she scares me."

44

But that wasn't really a mean thing to say, and nothing happened to spoil the afternoon. The only thing that would have made it more perfect would have been a card or a present from her own father, but she hadn't honestly expected that, so it wasn't too disappointing that nothing came.

She spent the evening reading and looking up a lot of new words in the Webster's; and when it was time for Shelly to go to sleep, Annabelle didn't tell her to turn off the light, so she read right up to nine o'clock.

Even when Jack left for Detroit in the morning, Annabelle remained cheerful and kind. She asked Laurie what she'd like for dinner that evening, and if she wouldn't like to get her hair cut. "That blue dress makes you look sort of cute, and the hair cut would be even cuter. Cooler, too, with summer coming up."

Laurie didn't care one way or the other about the hair, but she knew from past experience that when Annabelle wanted to do her a favor, she'd better agree to it. So she had her hair cut and was surprised to find that when it was short it waved, just a little, around her face. It *did* look nice, and Annabelle hugged her and said to Shelly, "Isn't Laurie pretty this way?"

Laurie would have enjoyed the hugging a lot more if she hadn't been so sure the affection would be short lived. She watched her step very carefully, so as not to do anything irritating; but Annabelle was in a good humor and nothing seemed able to spoil it.

Even when Laurie was cleaning her room and got the vacuum cleaner caught on a cord and tipped over a lamp and cracked it, Annabelle didn't hit her. Laurie tried not to cringe visibly when her mother appeared in the doorway after the sound of the crash died away; it was the habit of years to cringe inwardly, waiting for the blow to fall.

"Oh, Laurie, what happened? Darn, the base is cracked. Ask Tim for some of that model cement he uses, and we'll see if we can't put this little piece back in it."

So the lamp was fixed, and still Annabelle's humor held. Jack called on Thursday evening, and she talked to him gaily about the things she had been doing and told him the new place would be ready for them to move into over the weekend.

Laurie had had her stitches taken out by then, and while the scar was still prominent it didn't bother her much and she was back to washing dishes again. It made her stomach feel all tense and uncomfortable to think of moving, but there was nothing she could do about it.

It wouldn't be an apartment, this time, but half of a duplex. They had to explain to Shelly what a duplex was, half of a two-family house. There was a big yard, and in the other half of it lived a couple by the name of Gerrold.

"Maybe we could have a dog, if there's a yard," Tim said speculatively.

But Annabelle squelched that idea in a hurry. "No pets allowed. We're lucky to get in with three kids, since the Gerrolds seem to be very quiet people. You probably will still have to be quiet in the house, but it will be better there than here where there's no place to play."

"I like playing in the park," Tim said. Ordinarily Annabelle would have frowned at that, but this time she only laughed. "A back yard of your own is better than a park. You'll see."

The duplex, when they got there, on Friday afternoon, *was* nicer than the apartment. For one thing, there were four bedrooms, so Laurie got a room to herself. It wasn't very big, only large enough for a bed and a chest of drawers and a chair, but it was private.

Shelly's room was even smaller, for it held only a bed and a chest, with no room for a chair unless she'd climbed over it to get into bed, but she, too, seemed pleased to have a room of her own.

Tim got the largest of the three small bedrooms upstairs, because his model collection needed space. He was generous, though, and offered to let Shelly set up her tea table there, with the little red chairs, if she promised not to touch his models.

Best of all was the yard. Even Laurie had to admit she liked the yard. It wasn't an ordinary city lot backyard, but one that plunged into a ravine at the back, a ravine that was woodsy and had a small creek running through the bottom of it. There were wild flowers along its banks, and so many trees and bushes that it would be easy to find a hiding place when she wanted to be alone.

Shelly was not intrigued with the woodsy ravine. The sandbox near the house was more to her liking.

"All the better," Tim observed to Laurie with satisfaction. "More privacy for us, huh, Laurie?"

"The yard's fine," she agreed, but he read her lack of enthusiasm.

"What's the matter, then? Don't you like it?"

"I like the place all right. But Monday we're going to have to start at a new school. I hate starting at a new school."

"I don't like it, either," Tim admitted. "But it's only a month and school will be out. Then we can spend all our time out there in the woods. We can build a treehouse and a fort, and maybe if we build a dam across the creek, we can make a pond big enough to swim in. Well, big enough to get wet in, anyway."

She smiled. It was an idea. "I never had a brother to spend the summer with. Maybe it won't be so bad," she said.

But in her heart she was still dreading the new school, the new teacher, the strange kids who were always so hard to get acquainted with. And she missed the girls she had left behind. If she could make a friend or two before school was out, someone she could continue to see through vacation time, it would be some help. But she really wasn't any good at making friends. She couldn't walk up to a bunch of kids and ask if she could join them to eat lunch, or play in their games, or borrow a pencil. If they asked her first it was all right, but so often nobody did. Everyone simply ignored her, as if she were a fence post.

She knew she wasn't a very interesting sort of girl. She wasn't good at athletics. She was a fairly good student; that is to say, she did her lessons and got good grades on her tests. But she seldom spoke to anyone, unless someone asked her a question. So there wasn't much chance that she'd have any new friends.

And then, on Sunday afternoon, when Jack and Annabelle had taken the other kids and gone off to a movie Laurie didn't want to see, she discovered George.

Annabelle was always after her because she didn't eat enough, and said she'd look better if she weren't so skinny. Laurie wasn't sure why she didn't eat more, unless it was because mealtimes were uncomfortable for her. She had to sit close to Annabelle, never knowing what sort of humor she would be in, never knowing when she might strike out in anger.

But sometimes, when she was alone, Laurie got very hungry and fixed herself a good-sized lunch and ate it all. Like today. She made a peanut butter sandwich and selected a big red apple and took them out on the back steps to read in the sunshine while she ate.

49

The house had two stories, but it wasn't arranged with a flat on each level. Instead, it was like two two-story houses that had somehow become Siamese twins, fastened together in the middle, each like a mirror image of the other. In the front, there was a porch at each corner, far apart, so each family had its own entrance and a reasonable amount of privacy.

In the back, however, the porches were joined, with only a sort of fence between the two sections. Laurie hadn't seen either Mr. or Mrs. Gerrold yet, the people who lived in the other section of the house, and she didn't expect to see them now. Annabelle had said they were quiet.

So it was a surprise to find a boy who wasn't much older than she was sitting on the other half of the porch. Annabelle, Laurie thought, had taken pains to make sure that there were no children in the house. When Jack had laughingly protested at her statement that kids bothered her, when there were three in their own family, she had said she meant other people's kids, and insisted they'd all be better off where there wasn't a lot of racket. Annabelle often had headaches and had to rest in the afternoons, and she couldn't control the amount of noise made by other people's kids.

The boy was quite ordinary looking, except that he had unusually large ears that stuck out from his head more than most people's. His hair was darker than Laurie's, a sort of light brown, and he had freckles across his face.

He sat in a chair, whittling on a stick. Not making anything, just cutting off long slivers that fell in a pile around his feet. He looked up when Laurie came out the door and said, "Hi."

Startled, she said, "Hi."

"My name's George. What's yours?"

"Laurie."

George needed a haircut. He shoved the hair out of his eyes, but it immediately fell right back. "I thought there were just the little kids I saw out here last night."

"That's Tim and Shelly. They're my stepbrother and sister."

"Which one's your stepparent, then? Your mother or your father?"

"Jack's my stepfather."

George had stopped whittling, as if he were really interested. "Do you like him?"

"He's all right," Laurie said cautiously. "Do you live here? We thought there was a couple without any children living here."

George grinned. He had extraordinarily large front teeth. "Well, most of the time they've been here, I've been in a hospital, so probably nobody knew they had me. That's why they moved here, to be close to the hospital. We've got a house of our own, but it's too far away for them to be able to see me if they had to drive back and forth."

Laurie bit into her sandwich and chewed thoughtfully. He must have been in the hospital quite a while if they'd moved because of it. She wondered what had been the matter with him but didn't quite like to ask. She remembered how she'd felt sometimes when people asked her about her injuries.

"It's a nice yard here," she contributed after a small silence. She didn't feel as if he were forcing her to talk; but for once she felt like saying something. "Don't you like it down by the creek? Tim . . . that's my brother . . . says maybe we can build a dam and make a swimming pool."

"I've never been down there," George said, cutting deeply enough into the stick to divide it in two. "Is it a big creek?"

Astonished, Laurie momentarily just looked at him. "How come you haven't been there? Did you just get out of the hospital?"

"No. I've been out almost a month, but until the last few days I haven't been outside." He reached over suddenly and pulled up the legs of his jeans. Laurie drew in a small breath when she saw metal braces on legs thinner than her own. "These aren't much good for walking. I mean, I can stand up, if I hang onto something, but I have to use crutches to do any more than that. My mother doesn't think I should go down in the woods on crutches. Maybe I'll try it, though, if it's a really neat creek."

She pulled her gaze forcibly away from the braces. "Were you in an accident?"

"No. I've got a bone disease. I've had four operations so far. Maybe when I quit growing, it'll stabilize. You know, so I won't have to keep on having operations. What grade are you in?"

"I'll be going into the sixth next year."

"Me, too. I should be in the seventh, but I missed so much school because of being in the hospital that I got behind. I'm going to have a home teacher, and maybe I can catch up, but I'll probably have to have lessons all summer." He made a face. "What book are you reading?"

"A library book. It's called *The Headless Cupid*. It's a mystery."

"I like mysteries, too. And adventure stories, and books about dogs. I like dogs. I've got one, a collie named Dusty, but we couldn't bring him here. He's on my uncle's farm until I get well enough to go back home. You like dogs?"

"I never had one. My mother doesn't like dogs."

George nodded understandingly. "I really missed Dusty while I was in the hospital. It isn't that the people there don't like dogs, but they're unsanitary. The dogs are, I mean." He grinned again and pulled at one of his large ears. Laurie wondered if that was why they stuck out so far, because he pulled on them.

The afternoon wore on, and it wasn't until she heard the family returning that Laurie realized she hadn't read at all. She'd just sat on the back step talking to George, in a way she couldn't remember ever doing before with anyone. Just as if they were friends, she and George.

54

But instinct told her to keep the friendship a secret. So she didn't mention George to anyone, not even to Tim when he came home.

Starting school was every bit as bad as she'd thought it would be. Annabelle said they were plenty big enough to go by themselves, and they had records from the other school, so Laurie and Tim walked the six blocks to the new place.

Everything was quite different from what they were used to. Laurie had been through the routine before, going up a strange walk, being stared at by strange kids, feeling unable to smile back even if some of them seemed friendly. But it never seemed to get any easier to do.

The first day Laurie got lost twice. She'd never gone to a school where they had to change rooms with each class, and the second time it was all she could do not to cry. And wouldn't that have been absurd for someone who was eleven years old!

She was supposed to go to a music class, but she couldn't find the music room until she asked an older girl in the hall. She found it then, but the class had already started, and the kids all stared at her when she walked in.

The teacher's name was on the blackboard: Miss Mullen. Miss Mullen was young and pretty and dressed the way Annabelle did when she was going out somewhere special. She turned toward the doorway and said, "Yes? Did you want something?"

Laurie swallowed. "I'm . . . I'm supposed to go to the fifth grade music class. Is this the right place?"

"Yes, it is." Miss Mullen had a lovely smile. "Take a book and find a seat, and after class I'll get your name. All right?"

Once everybody stopped looking at her and opened their music books, Laurie forgot to be self-conscious and enjoyed the singing. And at the close of the class Miss Mullen not only entered her name on the record book, she stopped another girl and asked her to show Laurie where the next class was. Laurie felt a warm glow of appreciation.

That was the only nice thing that happened, though. She told Tim about it on the way home. He got out half an hour earlier than the fifth graders, but he was hanging around the front door when she went out.

"I thought I'd wait and see how you made out. Boy, have I got a strict teacher!" he said, kicking at a tuft of grass as they set off toward home. "This one kid talked back, and she nearly twisted his ear off! I sat behind him, and it stayed red for an hour! I guess I won't sass Mrs. Potter!"

Laurie twisted to look at him, trotting along beside her. "Do you usually? Sass teachers?"

Tim grinned. "No, but sometimes I want to. Did you get a good teacher?"

"I got five teachers, or is it six? I don't think I'm going to like the P.E. teacher. I forget her name, but she thinks everybody ought to be an athlete, but I'm not, and there's just no way I'm ever going to be a ballplayer. But my music teacher's nice, Miss Mullen. She's pretty, too."

They walked home, and Laurie was glad he'd waited for her. She wondered what it would have been like, all these years, if she'd had a brother of her own. She might not have been quite so lonely when they moved all the time. But of course Tim wasn't quite nine years old, so he couldn't talk to her the way someone her age would.

Thinking that reminded her of George, and her step quickened. Maybe George would be out on the back steps again this afternoon.

She didn't get to find out, though. Annabelle had a headache and was lying down. She'd left a note for Laurie about starting supper, so there wasn't a chance to go out in the backyard at all.

Annabelle's headache was not a good sign. When her head hurt, Annabelle began to get snappish, and everybody walked carefully.

Not that she ever touched Shelly or Tim. Maybe she was afraid of what Jack would do, if she hurt his children. Certainly they wouldn't hesitate to tell him, Laurie thought, if she ever hit one of them with a knife. What would he do? she wondered. Jack didn't like scenes and often gave in rather than prolong an argument, even when it was obvious he thought he was right. But he seemed to really like his kids, and Laurie didn't think he'd tolerate anyone mistreating them.

How would he react if he knew about the things Annabelle did to *her?* It wasn't the first time she'd speculated on that, of course. He'd never been there when anything happened; but what if she went up to him when he came home and said, "My mother deliberately cut me with a knife today because she was angry with me?"

Naturally it wouldn't be the same as if it happened to his *own* kids. He thought she was a funny girl, an odd one he didn't understand. But he was kind, if you didn't let yourself be scared by his loud voice. He'd found out what she'd wanted most for her birthday, and he'd spent a lot of money on it. Would he tell Annabelle to stop doing things to hurt her own daughter?

But of course, Annabelle wouldn't just stand there and let Laurie tell her story without offering her own version, the way she did with the doctors and the nurses and the teachers. She'd remind him of how careless Laurie was and how clumsy, and probably she'd even say Laurie was lying.

If she did that, who would he believe?

That was where the tiny thread of hope snapped right off, as if it had been cut with a scissor. Because if she said one thing and Annabelle said something else, it would be Annabelle who was believed.

Maybe Grandma Denvers would have believed Laurie (although that didn't necessarily mean she'd have done anything about it), because she knew her daughter as well as anyone did and had seen her in a fit of temper throw a glass across the room so that it shattered against the wall.

But Jack had never seen his wife do anything like that. She sometimes got cross when he didn't do what she wanted, but she never yelled or swore or threw things. She certainly never hit him with anything. So if it came to that, he'd believe what she said and think Laurie was making up lies.

There was no refuge in Jack.

There was no refuge anywhere, except within herself. Laurie had come to terms with that situation a long time ago. It helped, some, to have her own room now. It was easier to get away from everyone else, to stay out of Annabelle's way, to withdraw into a world of make-believe in her books.

But always she knew it was pretending. She knew that outside her own door lurked the real world . . . and for eleven years her real world had been Annabelle.

Nell came to visit that evening, to see the new house. It was farther away from where she lived, and she didn't get there until almost time for Shelly to go to bed.

She looked around the living room. "Yes, it's nice," she said in response to Annabelle's nervous query. "But no nicer than where you were. I can't imagine moving if I didn't have to. It's such a lot of work."

"The children like it better here," Annabelle said brightly.

"Do they?" Nell's voice was dry. "Laurie never stirs out of her chair with her book, so I wouldn't think it would matter to her. And Tim loved playing ball with the boys in the park."

"He'll meet new boys here." Some of the brightness faded.

"Yes, Tim's fairly self-reliant. I shouldn't have thought Laurie was the sort to make friends easily, though. Seems to me she'd have been happier staying where she was, at least until school was out."

Laurie, sitting in the recliner that was Jack's when he was home, her finger marking the word she was looking up in the enormous dictionary in her lap, felt a surge of gratitude. Imagine an elderly lady like Nell realizing how difficult it was for her to change schools.

"It was a family decision," Annabelle said. She didn't sound exactly hostile, but Laurie knew how she felt just under the surface. "For the good of all of us."

"Yes, of course," Nell said, her tone leaving no one in doubt as to what she *really* thought. "Well, I hope you'll all be happy here, of course. I was glad when you had the Lessing Street apartment because it was so handy for me, and that's selfish of me, I guess. I don't mean to make a nuisance of myself, but it's lonesome without Jack's father, and I do enjoy my only grandchildren."

"You're always welcome, naturally." Annabelle sounded stiff. "By all means make yourself at home with the kids. I hope you'll excuse me if I go back to bed; I've had a migraine all day."

The atmosphere was different after Annabelle went away. Tim and Shelly talked to their grandmother, and after a while Nell took Shelly on her lap and read her a story. Nell didn't say much to Laurie, only smiled at her, but it was nice to be included as if they were all part of one family. If only her *own* grandmother had been like Nell . . .

It was Nell who put Shelly to bed. After she had gone, and Tim, too, had fallen asleep, Laurie took her own bath and washed her hair. She stood in front of the mirror, wondering how she would look if she curled her hair. It had a faint natural wave; maybe it wouldn't take much to make it look pretty nice.

She got out the pink curlers Annabelle used, and awkwardly set about rolling up her hair. She'd seen it done many times, but it wasn't as easy to do as she'd thought it would be. The curlers kept sliding out, and the ends kept sticking up so she had to do them over again. But she finally got it all done. Now if they didn't hurt her head when she went to bed . . .

"What are you doing?"

The voice was sharp, and Laurie spun around, knocking over the plastic container with the rest of the curlers. They flew all over the room, into the bathtub and the toilet, across the floor. One of them rolled up against Annabelle's slippered foot.

"I . . . I thought I'd try . . ."

Laurie stopped, for she recognized the murderous

rage in Annabelle's face. She had seen it often enough.

Jack wouldn't think Annabelle was pretty if he could see her now. Her mouth was flat and tight and angry.

"You *know* I've got one of these terrible headaches. You know how wretched they make me feel. But do you care? No, you don't! You don't care how much noise you make in here, disturbing me and making my head even worse! And look at the mess you've made! Clean it up and take my curlers out of your hair! I need them all myself!"

Annabelle never did her hair when she had a headache, but Laurie reached up a trembling hand to remove the first one, anyway. Her mother reached out as if to help her, but instead of removing the little pins that held the curls in place, she jerked curler, hair and all, so that Laurie let out a yelp of pain. And then Annabelle's hand came around in a hard blow against Laurie's cheek as she exploded in low-voiced fury.

"Don't make a lot of racket and wake up the other kids! Clean up this mess and then get to bed! You're just like your father, never have any consideration for anyone else, even when they're sick! Go on, clean it up!"

Eyes blurred, head stinging where the hair had nearly been pulled out, Laurie bent over to pick up the nearest of the curlers on the floor. And Annabelle kicked her.

Kicked her hard, hard enough to send her sprawling, hitting her mouth against the edge of the bathtub. Laurie felt a tooth go through her lip, tasted the blood in her mouth, knew the old, familiar terror and helplessness.

She was almost unaware of the blows that rained on her back as she crouched on the floor, her hand to her mouth, watching the blood run down her arm and into the tub. She just closed her eyes and waited until it was over.

Annabelle was gasping for breath, finally, as if she'd been running. She rummaged in the medicine chest for a bottle of pills, shook two of them into her hand, and took them with a glass of water. She didn't look around as Laurie slowly got to her feet.

Laurie waited until her mother had left the bathroom before she got a washcloth and bathed her mouth. The blood was slowing, but there was a bluish bruise on her chin where she'd hit the tub, and the cut on her lip hurt like anything. She couldn't see any way she could put a bandage on it.

She spit out the blood that had run inside her mouth, and rinsed with cold water. Her legs were shaking and she felt sick to her stomach, the way she often did after one of these episodes.

Why did Annabelle do it?

Other kids did things wrong, made mistakes, were far naughtier than Laurie could ever remember being. They might be punished, made to stay in their rooms or miss meals or even get spanked. But their mothers didn't do them physical harm. So why did Annabelle do it?

That she looked like her father, and that Annabelle hated him, wasn't reason enough. Laurie knew a number of kids whose parents were divorced and didn't like each other at all, but they didn't hate their kids only because they looked like the opposite parent.

It wasn't just that Annabelle had a headache, either, Laurie thought as she put the curlers away. Sometimes Annabelle did things like this when there wasn't a thing wrong with her except that she was "nervous." Laurie felt she herself was nervous all the time, practically, waiting to be attacked in some way, yet she didn't react by striking out against whoever happened to be near her. And Annabelle always had enough control not to do things like this when there were any witnesses.

"Laurie?" Tim whispered from the darkened hallway.

She turned, dropping the cloth from her rapidly swelling lip, to meet his dark eyes.

"Jeepers, Laurie, what happened?"

Laurie said nothing, replacing the washcloth.

"Are you OK?"

She nodded, turning back to the sink to rinse out the cloth. The water that ran down the drain was pink.

"Did she . . . did *she* do it?"

Again Laurie didn't answer, but she didn't have

to. Tim glanced over his shoulder, but the bedroom door remained closed. He put his hand on Laurie's arm.

"Come on," he said. "I'll walk upstairs with you. Is it all right now?"

She was grateful for his support, even though she couldn't talk to him about it. They went upstairs, and Tim whispered, "Good night," and she got into bed. She was still trembling, and the lip hurt, and it was going to look terrible in the morning.

She wanted to cry, but somehow, this time, she couldn't even do that. Somewhere out there in the wide world, maybe in California or New York or some other far away place, was Harry Kolman, her father. Didn't her anguish reach him? Didn't he feel anything, when she lay here in the dark wishing so desperately that she knew where he was, wishing he would come and rescue her?

She knew what Annabelle would say. "He doesn't care about you, Laurie. He never did, he never will. So forget about him."

But she couldn't forget, because he was the only hope she had. And she had to continue hoping things would get better or she would just die. *Please, please*, she begged silently up into the darkness. *Help me. Help me.*

But there was no answer.

FOUR

SHE KNEW BEFORE SHE EVER looked in the mirror that she was a mess. She went downstairs, her lip swollen and sore, and forced herself to walk into the kitchen.

Annabelle was apparently over her headache because she was cooking bacon and eggs. She gave them cereal when she didn't feel well, or even let them fix their own breakfasts.

She turned around and saw Laurie standing there. For a moment Laurie thought she flinched, or at least that there was something, some recognition of what she had done, there in her face.

"Good heavens. You're going to have to go to

school looking like that!"

As if Laurie had done it herself, through her own stupidity or carelessness!

Tim looked up from the table, a rim of white around his mouth as he set his milk down. He wiped at it with a paper napkin. "I wouldn't go to school if I got hurt like that," he stated flatly.

Laurie felt a flicker of alarm, for it was a challenge, flung straight at Annabelle. Did he mean her to realize that he knew she had been the one that did it? Laurie tried to signal to him with her eyes; it wasn't safe to do this.

But Annabelle didn't pick up the challenge, as she would certainly have done if Laurie had spoken like that. She slid an egg onto his plate and said, "Eat your breakfast. Come on, Laurie, it's ready."

Eating was not easy; Laurie discovered very quickly that salt made the puncture inside her mouth sting and tears came to her eyes. But she knew enough not to say she wanted to stay home. It wouldn't even be true. She didn't want to go to school, but she didn't want to stay home with her mother, either.

Shelly came staggering down the stairs in her pajamas, rubbing her sleepy eyes. She slid into the chair beside her brother and then noticed Laurie across the table.

"What's the matter with your face, Laurie? Did you hurt it?"

Laurie couldn't speak. She drank milk, hoping it

would wash away the stinging salt, so it was Annabelle who replied.

"She bumped herself, Shelly. Do you want an egg, too?"

There were some boys ahead of them going to school, boys about Tim's age, and one of them waved at him, but he didn't try to catch up with them. Instead, he walked along with Laurie, his hands jammed into his pockets.

"There must be something you can do," he said. "Nobody should have to just stand there and let someone hurt them, all for nothing. You didn't do anything, did you?"

"I used her curlers. And she said I made noise . . ." Only she hadn't made any noise, not really. Only the running water made any sound, and she was expected to take a bath, so washing her hair hadn't made any difference.

"She's mean! She's the most terrible, mean person I know! Laurie, why don't you tell my dad? He wouldn't let her do things like that to you!"

"But I'm her kid, not his. And besides," it always came back to the same thing, "she'd say it was my own fault, and he'd believe her. It's what she always tells the people at the hospital, and they always believe her."

"Why should they believe her instead of you?"

"Because she's a grown-up," Laurie said; and while Tim grumbled all the way to school, he couldn't come up with anything to change that.

She hated walking down the hallway, because people looked at her. She didn't know anyone in this school, yet, so no one asked her what had happened, but everybody looked at her swollen and discolored lip and chin, and she knew they were wondering.

"Good morning, Laurie," someone said cheerfully, and she turned to see Miss Mullen coming out of the principal's office. She was wearing a bright orange sweater and a brown skirt, and she looked very pretty. She was smiling until she saw Laurie's face. "Golly, what happened to you?"

There it was again. And suddenly Laurie felt an overwhelming impulse to tell the truth. Not to say she'd slipped and fallen and bumped herself, but to say, "My mother did it." Miss Mullen was a nice person, and she liked Laurie. Mightn't she believe it?

Her mouth was dry and her heart hammered so that she actually put up a hand to push against it where it tried to break through her ribs. She remembered how brutal Annabelle could be when she was crossed, and the fear was almost more than she could bear. The boy who had spoken to her on the bleachers had said there was no use in asking for help, but maybe he was wrong. Maybe there was a chance someone like Miss Mullen could do something to help.

But, if she couldn't, if Annabelle found out she'd told. . . . No, Laurie thought. She couldn't allow herself to think of the consequences if it went wrong. She couldn't worry about how much worse it could be;

she had to hope for the best that *might* be, if Miss Mullen believed her.

She wouldn't lie to this teacher, not this time.

She opened her mouth, her lip stretching painfully, her tongue so frozen she wasn't sure she *could* speak, and said, "Please, could I . . . could I talk to you alone?"

Miss Mullen's hand came down on her shoulder, a gentle, comforting hand. "Why, of course, Laurie. We'll have to run now, there goes the bell. But I have some time free right after school. Why don't you come to my room then, all right?"

Then she was gone, moving down the hall toward the music room, and Laurie was jostled by hurrying students, suddenly unable to move, appalled at what she had done.

She had committed herself to telling Miss Mullen the truth about Annabelle.

The day drew out into the longest one she could ever remember. She alternated between determination to tell the truth, everything that Annabelle had done to her, and terror that she wouldn't be able to go through with it.

She was a coward. She knew she was a coward. Yet wasn't it, perhaps, even more cowardly to go on the way she was, just waiting for Annabelle to fly into one of her rages and strike out with whatever came to hand first?

She should have felt better, having made the first

move toward Miss Mullen. Only she didn't. She felt sick, sick with worry. She stumbled when she tried to read aloud in English class; she, who prided herself on her reading ability, couldn't even keep her place, and the teacher finally asked her to sit down while all the kids turned around and stared at her.

During arithmetic she was so nervous she thought she might have to ask to leave the room. When Miss Savage called on her, Laurie didn't even hear the question and only sat there, her face flushed, unable to say anything.

Miss Savage wasn't cross, though. She walked up the aisle between the seats and touched a hand to Laurie's forehead. "Are you feeling all right, Laurie?" she asked.

The heat in her face increased as she became the center of attention once more, with eyes watching her from every direction. She attempted to deny illness, but in truth she felt terrible, as if she might throw up any minute.

"I'm going to write you out a pass, and you take it to the nurse's office," Miss Savage said. "Do you know where it is? Right across from the principal's office in the main corridor?"

Laurie didn't want to see the nurse, but the pass had to be signed and eventually brought back, she knew. She paused on the way for a drink from the fountain, which was a mistake because it made her feel even more like throwing up.

The nurse's office was very small, and it had five

kids in it already. Two boys were giggling behind their hands and didn't look as if they had much the matter with them. Another older boy held a wet paper towel to a bleeding nose and a kindergartener with a skinned knee sat crying quietly while a friend tried to comfort her.

Laurie stood uncertainly just inside the door, waiting for the nurse to notice her. There was no place to sit down.

The nurse turned from the desk and nodded at her, neither friendly nor unfriendly, only very busy. "I'll be with you in a minute. Here, Thomas, hold your nose like this, very hard. I'm going to set the timer for five minutes, and you're to hold it tight until the timer goes off, you understand? Don't release it too soon or it will start bleeding again."

The boy with the bloody nose nodded to show that he understood and propped himself against the wall, watching the timer. The little girl with the skinned knee was the next one to be ministered to.

One of the giggling boys spoke out as the knee was being cleaned with antiseptic. "We was here first."

"Well, you aren't bleeding. We take care of the most urgent cases first around here," the nurse said pleasantly. "So sit still and don't make a nuisance of yourself."

It was several minutes before she got around to Laurie, who by that time had gone pale. "What seems to be the trouble?" The nurse looked at the slip Miss Savage had given her. "Running a fever? You don't feel like it, but let's check." She shook down a thermometer and stuck it in Laurie's mouth.

Maybe she should pretend that she was really sick, and they'd let her go home, Laurie thought. She looked bad enough to belong at home. Only then she wouldn't be here after school, and she wouldn't get to talk to Miss Mullen.

"Ninety-eight six," the nurse said briskly, checking the thermometer. "Perfectly normal. How are you feeling?"

"All right," Laurie said in a small voice. Annabelle was at home, and she'd be perturbed if Laurie were sent out of school. "I don't need to go home."

"Sure?" The nurse looked down at the bruised face and split lip. "You sure bumped yourself, didn't you? Or did you get hit with a ball or something?"

Laurie shook her head. She might have told the nurse the truth, since she was going to tell Miss Mullen after school anyway, but how could she, with all these other kids listening in?

"Well, you don't appear to have anything contagious. You want to go back to class?"

Laurie nodded, and the nurse signed her pass. But she didn't go back to arithmetic, not right away. She went into the girls' bathroom and wondered how she'd ever get through the day until three thirty. She felt like crying, but that would only make it worse, because then everyone would wonder what she'd

74

been crying about. She knew from experience that bathing her eyes with wet paper towels didn't eliminate the redness, not for a long time.

A girl came in, one who was in her music class. Laurie thought her name was Sally. She looked at Laurie curiously.

"You all right?"

"Yes," Laurie said around the lump in her throat, although it wasn't true.

The girl's hand was bleeding. "I knocked my wart off, and Mrs. Hammond was very annoyed with me." She ran water over the spot. "I can't help it if it gets knocked off, can I? But they always think if there's anything the matter with you, it's your own fault."

Laurie would have liked to make some encouraging reply, but she couldn't think of anything to say. Sometimes her brain worked all right; why did she have so much trouble thinking up a few simple sentences in situations like this?

Apparently discouraged by Laurie's lack of response, the other girl didn't say any more, but patted her hand dry with a paper towel and walked out.

It didn't matter, Laurie told herself. Even if she'd made a friend of this girl (although how could she do that in just a few minutes?), it wouldn't matter. Because before they got to be best friends, Annabelle would find a way to spoil it, the way she always did.

When she finally returned to the classroom,

nobody bothered her any more that day. And then it was time for school to be out, and she felt her fears rising again as she made her way against the traffic in the hall toward the music room. How would she say it, so that she would be believed? Would it help if she told which hospital she'd been taken to, when Annabelle had slashed her with the knife? Would anyone look at the records and see that she'd been there before, with a burn, and a fractured arm from the time she'd been pushed down the stairs? Would those things matter now?

She turned the knob, but the door refused to open. The music room was locked.

There was a tall narrow window in each of the doors. Laurie pressed her face against this one and peered inside, but the room was empty. Where was Miss Mullen? She couldn't have forgotten! Laurie thought in a burst of despair.

She waited for nearly half an hour, but no one came. And at last, when the janitor came along the hall with his big broom, she had to admit that there wasn't much chance Miss Mullen would be as late as this.

Slowly, Laurie walked home, long after everyone else had gone. She was past even crying.

Tim met her in the kitchen. He was building a sandwich of cheese and mustard and lettuce and mayonnaise and salami. "Annabelle's taken Shelly out to buy her some shoes. She said you were to turn on the oven at three forty-five, but you weren't here, so I did it."

"Thank you," Laurie said. She went upstairs and changed into her everyday clothes, pausing for a moment to examine her reflection in the mirror. It was no wonder the teacher had sent her to the nurse; she looked terrible.

She didn't want anything to eat. She didn't even want to read any of her library books. She thought maybe she'd go down by the creek, all by herself.

But when she went out onto the back porch, George was there. It was as if he'd been waiting for her.

"Hi. Did you have to stay after school today?"

Laurie turned to meet his friendly grin. "Yes, I . . . was supposed to talk to one of the teachers, but I guess she forgot. She didn't come."

"I'm getting a home teacher for the last few weeks of school. And then during the summer a guy from high school is going to tutor me," George said. "Listen, if I take my crutches, will you show me the creek?"

Laurie was somewhat dubious about that, since the embankment was fairly steep. But George insisted he could manage stairs, which couldn't be any worse than the bank, so they went out across the yard and into the trees.

Actually, George could move just about as quickly as she could.

"I've had a lot of practice," he told her. "I've been using them for almost two years, all the time they'd let me out of bed. It's kind of hard getting over fallen logs, though."

"Come around this end," Laurie told him, and found the easiest way to go.

The creek was clear and cold and sort of chuckled to itself as it meandered over the little rocks and around the tree roots. She felt better down here. George didn't say anything about her split lip and the bruises on her face, and after a while she forgot about them herself.

George couldn't take off his shoes and socks and wade because of the braces, but Laurie did, and then they started building a dam with rocks and bits of bark and broken branches. She had to do most of the hauling, and George did the engineering, as he called the planning of it.

It had to be done exactly right, or the water would carry away the brush they put across it. When the branches and bark were anchored by rocks, though, they stayed in place and the water began to build up behind the dam.

"It'll take a few more days to make a good pond," George said as they rested. "Maybe we could come down all day Saturday and work on it. Do you think your brother will want to help?"

It was then they heard Annabelle calling from the yard above them. Laurie yelled, "Coming!" and they started back up the bank.

Laurie hoped Annabelle would go inside before they reached the top, but she didn't. She was still standing there, her face expressionless, as the two of them came out of the woods.

"See you tomorrow, maybe," George said and hauled himself on his crutches up the steps and into the other half of the duplex.

Annabelle waited at the top of the back steps. Her gaze had followed George, but now it was fastened on Laurie's face.

"Who is *he*?" Her tone was mild, but Laurie wasn't deceived by that.

"His name is George," she said. Why hadn't she asked him to wait until she'd gone inside before he came up the hill? But on the other hand, how could she have done that? What if he'd had trouble getting up the steep bank on his crutches? And what would he have thought of such a request?

Laurie hesitated, wondering if she should tell an outright lie, and then decided that it wasn't worth the risk. Annabelle was bound to find out. "He lives here."

Annabelle hesitated in the doorway, indignation brightening her eyes. "But I understood there were no children in the other half of the house!"

"He's been in the hospital. He isn't here much." She moved quickly to wash her hands and set the table for dinner, hoping to use Annabelle's own tactic of changing the subject. "Do you want me to use the good plates tonight?"

"No, why would we use them when there's only you kids and me? What's the matter with the boy? Why can't he walk?"

"He has a bone disease. He's had a lot of operations." Laurie tried again. "Could I make lemonade, instead of having milk?"

"Stop trying to sidetrack me. What were you doing down there in the ravine with him?"

Laurie had trouble controlling her voice, making it sound natural and unconcerned, because she was fighting both apprehension and anger. Other people had friends; why was it so important to Annabelle that *she* never had any?

Even as the question formed in her mind, Laurie knew the answer. Annabelle herself was safer if she isolated Laurie, kept her away from people who might learn how she was mistreated and, possibly, attempt to do something about it.

"We were just playing," she said. She dropped a handful of silverware and stooped to pick it up, almost welcoming a blow if it meant getting Annabelle off the subject of George.

But there was no blow. Annabelle didn't even tell her to wash off the silverware.

"Playing what?"

Tim came into the kitchen, sizing up the situation at once. "Boy, am I hungry. What smells so good?" Annabelle ignored him. "Laurie, I asked you a question. Playing what?"

"We were building a dam," Laurie said. "Just piling things up to keep the water back, so it would make a pond."

"A pond! So Shelly can go down there and drown? Of all the stupid, dangerous things to do . . ."

"Shelly won't go down in the ravine," Tim said positively. "She's afraid of snakes."

"Are there snakes down there? I don't think you'd better go down there any more, Laurie."

"There aren't any snakes, I just told Shelly there were," Tim said. "So she'd stay up here in the yard where she belongs. Besides, she knows how to swim, if the pond gets big enough for that. Gram taught us to swim last summer when she took us to the beach for two weeks. Isn't dinner ready yet?"

He had finally succeeded in diverting Annabelle's attention, and she began to dish up the food; but Laurie knew that wouldn't be the end of it. Annabelle would never knowingly let her develop a close friendship with anyone.

FIVE

THE ENTIRE NEXT DAY WAS AN ordeal for Laurie. She hoped to spot Miss Mullen in the corridors, but there was no sign of her. Again Laurie steeled herself to talk to the teacher; during music class, she'd remind her that she wanted to speak to her alone, and maybe this time Miss Mullen wouldn't forget.

When she walked into the music room, however, there was no Miss Mullen at the front of the room. Instead, there was a heavyset older woman with a mannish haircut, who rapped sharply for order and told the stragglers to get to their seats.

What had happened to Miss Mullen?

As soon as the class quieted down, she found out.

The new teacher introduced herself.

"I'm Mrs. Sterling. As most of you probably know by now, Miss Mullen had an appendicitis attack yesterday and had to have surgery. So I'll be taking over her classes for the rest of the year. Now, we will open our books to page twelve."

The rest of the year! Miss Mullen wouldn't be back at all!

Laurie was so stricken that her mind refused to function. Only now did she realize how much she had counted on telling someone at last; how much hope she'd had that Miss Mullen could do something to help her. Her book lay forgotten in her lap until Mrs. Sterling rapped her across the knuckles with her stick.

"Page twelve, I said! Pay attention, please."

Everyone looked at Laurie, who turned a deep pink and rubbed unobtrusively at her stinging knuckles. She had to blink hard to keep back the tears, and she couldn't have said whether they were because of Miss Mullen or because her hand hurt.

She hoped Tim would be waiting for her, as he sometimes was after school, because she needed to talk to somebody; but today he had gone on home with the other boys. He wasn't even around when she got home. There was a note from Annabelle, held on the front of the refrigerator by little magnets, saying that she'd taken Shelly with her to her dental appointment, and that Laurie should turn on the oven at four thirty.

That meant she didn't dare go down into the

ravine, not until she'd started the oven for dinner. But when she looked out the back door, George was sitting on the steps, whittling at another stick.

"Hi," he said, as if he'd been waiting for her. "I went down today and worked a little more on the dam. I found some good logs to use, but I couldn't move them alone. You want to go see if we can do it together?"

She explained about Annabelle and the oven, so they just sat there in the spring sunshine, talking. And suddenly, without ever meaning to do so, she found herself telling George how she'd wanted to talk to Miss Mullen about a problem, and how disappointed she was that the teacher wouldn't be back.

"And the new teacher, this Mrs. Sterling, isn't the sort of person you'd tell anything to," George concluded.

"She wouldn't believe me, ever," Laurie said, shaking her head.

George nodded understandingly. "Do you always call your mother Annabelle?" he asked.

"I don't call her anything, to her face," Laurie admitted.

George hesitated, pulling on one of his large ears, and then asked quietly, "Did she do that to you? Hurt your face like that?"

Laurie's face flamed, but she didn't try to lie to him, the way she might have to someone else. "How did you know?"

"I don't know. Sort of guessed, from the way

you talk about her. And because you never said what happened. It isn't any of my business, but we're friends, aren't we? I won't tell anybody if you don't want me to."

"It would probably only make it worse, if she knew I told you. I was going to talk to Miss Mullen about it, but there isn't anyone else I'd tell."

"Why did she do it?"

It didn't even occur to Laurie to mention the curlers. She knew that wasn't what George was asking.

"She hates me because I'm like my father. He deserted us when I was little. I guess I look like him and act like him, and that makes her mad."

"George! Cookies are ready!" Mrs. Gerrold called from the kitchen next door. She stepped onto the porch, smiling when she saw that George was talking to Laurie. "Bring your friend along, if you like. Would you like a glass of milk, too?"

Except for the time she'd gone to Shirley's birthday party, it had been a long time since Laurie had been inside anyone else's house. She crossed the threshold gingerly, wondering if she ought to do it, with Annabelle liable to come home any minute.

But the good smells and the friendly attitude of George's mother proved too tempting. She edged inside the door and looked around with interest.

It was a pleasant, sunny kitchen, all painted yellow and with several kinds of food being prepared. Unlike Annabelle, who only really cooked when Jack was home, Mrs. Gerrold seemed to enjoy cooking. She had cookies on one end of the table, cooling in neat rows, and was just putting four loaves of bread into the oven.

"Better settle for two cookies each," she said, "so you won't spoil your suppers. You must be the Laurie that George has told us about."

Mrs. Gerrold didn't look anything like Annabelle. She wore jeans and a print blouse and tennis shoes, and her hair looked like she did it herself; but she had a lovely smile and friendly blue eyes, and her voice was soft and pleasant.

Laurie bit into the warm cookie, which was oatmeal with chocolate chips and raisins, both. It was big and chewy and delicious, and she ate it slowly, enjoying every crumb.

"I've been meaning to get over and say hello to your mother, but I can't seem to get around to it," Mrs. Gerrold said. She took some salad vegetables out of the refrigerator and began to clean them at the sink. "I guess she's busy too. I noticed her car was gone this afternoon."

"She's at the dentist," Laurie said, washing down the last of the cookie with some milk. George had already eaten both his cookies and sneaked a third while his mother wasn't looking, winking at Laurie as he did so.

"Nothing serious, I hope. We have to take George in for another checkup next week. Things like that take up so much time, don't they?"

"Can we have some carrot sticks?" George asked, and brought them back to the table, two apiece.

"They shouldn't spoil your dinners. Why don't you show Laurie your room, George? She might enjoy seeing your collections."

"I have to go turn on the oven," Laurie said. "In five minutes." She hesitated. "Then maybe I could come back."

She was taking a chance, she knew. If Annabelle found out about the visit, she wouldn't like it. Yet it was so good to be in there with them, in a home where people were calm and really seemed to care about each other. She turned on the oven and hurried back.

George had a room on the ground floor, because his mother thought he shouldn't have to manage the stairs on his crutches, although he said that he could go up and down them as fast as anyone else.

"But it's the biggest bedroom, so I didn't argue," he admitted. "I collect a lot of junk. It's what you can do when you have to stay in bed a lot. People know you like certain things, and they bring them to you for presents."

His "junk" included rocks, maps, and butterflies. He had all sorts of butterflies she'd never seen before.

"I used to collect those myself, outdoors back home, before I got sick," George told her. "And that rock, there, I found down in the ravine this morning. I think it's an agate."

But the collection Laurie found most fascinating was George's books. He had a lot of them, several hundred, anyway. She ran an admiring hand over the backs of the nearest ones.

"I read a lot. I like books better than TV, don't you? You can borrow any of them you want," George offered.

Looking at all his books and things, Laurie decided that George probably hadn't had much chance to make friends his own age, either, if he hadn't been to school for two years. The friends he'd had before that were somewhere else, where he'd lived before he got sick. That made her feel that they were closer, more friendly.

When she was ready to go home, Mrs. Gerrold was just taking the bread out of the oven, and the smell made Laurie's mouth water, even after having eaten two big cookies and the carrot sticks.

George's mother grinned at her. "Nothing smells better than fresh bread, does it? Here, I'll wrap this in waxed paper and you can take a loaf for your supper. How'll that be?"

Laurie stopped in consternation. She would love to have some of the hot bread, but she was afraid Annabelle wouldn't react the way Mrs. Gerrold thought she would.

"Oh, I couldn't . . . you cooked it for your-selves . . ."

"We've got three more loaves. And I'll bake some more when that's gone. Here you go. Unwrap it when you get it home, it's still too hot to be wrapped. You can bring the plate back tomorrow."

There was nothing for her to do but take the bread. As she went out the door with it, George called, "Let's get up early tomorrow and go to work on the dam, OK?"

She would have had trouble immediately when she got home except for one thing: Nell was there.

Annabelle had come in moments earlier, and the fragrance of the bread brought everybody to attention.

"What's that?" Annabelle demanded.

"Fresh bread." Laurie's voice quavered. "The lady next door thought we might like some. I didn't want to be impolite, so . . ."

"Smells marvelous," Nell commented. "I may invite myself to supper, just to get some of it."

Annabelle stood in the middle of the room, not saying anything for a moment, but there was a tell-tale twitch at the corner of her mouth.

"Yeah, stay for supper, Gram," Tim invited. "She can, can't she, Annabelle?"

Annabelle's words were stiff. "I only planned on having a small casserole of macaroni and cheese, and a salad."

"But with homemade bread there'll be enough to fill us all up, won't there?" Tim insisted. "Boy, does that smell great!"

Nell shot a knowing glance at her daughter-in-law. "I won't stay. I only wanted to leave these things I found today, play clothes. They were so inexpensive, I couldn't resist them, and I thought they'd all need shorts and tops with vacation coming up."

"Hey, Gram," Tim demanded, "are we going to get to spend our vacation with you again this year?"

"Well, not all of it. But I expect you could come for a month or so, if your father has no objections. And Annabelle, of course."

"You want to come too, Laurie?" Tim asked, as if he had the right to make such an invitation.

"Laurie has her own relatives to visit, if she wants to go somewhere," Annabelle said, turning abruptly away.

Her own relatives. Laurie hadn't seen any of them in ages; what few there were had been alienated years before by Annabelle, herself. Laurie might have liked going with Tim and Shelly to their grandmother's. They talked as if they always had a good time there.

Nell tightened her grasp on the handles of her purse. "Well, I'll run along. I hope this stuff fits, because it was on sale and I can't take it back. See you later, kids."

Tim and Shelly went to the front door with her to say good-bye. Annabelle stood in the middle of the kitchen and glared at the offending loaf of bread. "Why is she giving us food? Does she think we can't feed ourselves? Or that I can't cook?"

Annabelle never baked bread. Lots of people

didn't, Laurie knew; bread was sort of tricky to make. But almost everyone liked to *eat* it, and she knew Mrs. Gerrold had only been making a friendly gesture.

She also knew there was no explaining this to Annabelle. She stood by, helplessly, as her mother moved around the room, slamming drawers and banging pans to express her annoyance with this woman next door.

"What were you doing over there, anyway?" Annabelle suddenly demanded, just about the time Laurie hoped she was getting over her bad temper.

"Just . . . talking to George." Laurie's mouth went dry, the way it did when she knew Annabelle was upset.

"Well, don't go over there any more. There's nothing more annoying than having the neighbor kids running in and out of your house; I won't have you causing problems with the people next door by tracking into their place."

Laurie said nothing. She knew Mrs. Gerrold had been happy to have her there with George, but maybe Annabelle honestly couldn't understand that.

Annabelle didn't eat any of the bread at dinner-time, but Tim and Shelly not only ate several slices each, Tim kept saying how good it was. Laurie knew better than to do that; she ate her share, thickly spread with butter, but she kept still about it.

While Laurie did the dishes, alone in the kitchen, she let her mind create a story, the way she often did. She imagined coming out of school in the afternoon and finding a tall, fair-haired man watching her from a big car parked near the curb. She wouldn't be frightened of him, though, because she'd know at once who he was, even though she hadn't seen him since she was three years old.

He'd grin and say, "Hi, Laurie, remember me?" And then they'd sit in the car and talk, and he'd tell her all about what he'd been doing, traveling around the country all these years, and he'd explain that he hadn't gotten in touch with her because they'd moved so often he hadn't been able to find her.

And then he'd say, "But now that we're together again, how would you like to go out to Colorado with me? I've got a ranch out there, with horses to ride and everything. You're big enough to choose who you want to live with, and since you've been with Annabelle for eight years, maybe you'd like to live with me for a while now?"

And she'd say yes, of course, and when they went to tell Annabelle she'd be furious (or maybe she wouldn't, maybe she'd be glad to be rid of the responsibility), but Laurie's father wouldn't stand for any nonsense. He'd help Laurie pack her things, and they'd go off together in the big car to Colorado.

She'd got as far as learning to ride on the ranch when she was startled by the voice right beside her ear. She hadn't known anyone was in the room with her, and when Annabelle said, "Let me run some water so I can take an aspirin," Laurie jumped.

The plate she was holding slid out of her hand and hit on the divider between the sinks; in dismay, she watched it crack into three pieces and slide into the rinse water where the suds floated to the top in hundreds of tiny bubbles.

"Laurie, for heaven's sake!" It was easy to tell when Annabelle had another of her headaches coming on. Her tone always went up a notch. "Those are the plates I got for a wedding gift! Why can't you be more careful?"

Laurie didn't say anything. She knew better. It never did any good, and sometimes it just made Annabelle madder.

Her mother ran a glass of water and swallowed the white tablets in her hand, then stared angrily at the broken china. "Well, take them out and throw them away before somebody gets cut on them. Honestly, I can't believe how much like your father you are, never care what you do to someone else's valuables, never care if something's important to me! The older you get, the more you're like Harry Kolman. Sometimes you're so much like him I think I could kill you!"

Never, in all the terrible years, had Annabelle said anything like that before.

Laurie, paralyzed, stood looking into her mother's face, and she read the truth written there. In agony she whirled, not bothering to wipe the suds off her hands, forgetting about the broken plate, and ran out the back door and across the yard.

She heard Annabelle's voice calling after her, but she ran on, plunging down into the ravine, tripping over a root and sprawling, then scrambling up and dashing on.

The second time she fell, she was nearly at the bottom. Her left wrist twisted under her, and the pain of it made her gasp for breath. She'd fallen on the edge of the creek; when she was able to sit up and move her hand experimentally, she decided it was only sprained rather than broken, and she dabbled it in the water, welcoming the coolness.

She couldn't go on this way, Laurie thought with a quiet desperation that ruled out tears. She couldn't spend the rest of her life being terrified that one day Annabelle would, in a final burst of uncontrolled rage, actually kill her. Not just cut her or burn her or disable her in some way, but permanently cripple or kill her.

If only Miss Mullen hadn't gotten sick. She could have talked to Miss Mullen, she was sure she could have. Perhaps there was another teacher she could talk to, someone who would believe her . . .

Up above, at the top of the hill, she could hear Annabelle, calling her.

Laurie crouched there beside the small creek, cradling her sprained wrist, while her body was wracked with spasms like sobs, except that there were no tears.

What am I going to do? she asked silently.

And, as always before, there was no answer.

SIX

"LAURIE? WHAT ON EARTH'S HAP-pened? Are you hurt?"

For a moment she froze, hunched over there on the ground, and then she realized the voice was not Annabelle's.

Laurie lifted her head and saw Mrs. Gerrold and George, coming along the floor of the ravine toward her. At the same time, they all heard Annabelle calling and the sounds she made as she pushed through the underbrush, making her way down the bank.

Annabelle reached her only moments after the Gerrolds did and came to a halt beside her, panting slightly with the exertion.

"I think she fell and twisted her wrist," Mrs. Gerrold said. "That bank is too steep for running. It isn't broken, is it, Laurie?"

There was a pain in her chest far greater than the one in her wrist. So great that Laurie couldn't even try to speak. She'd rather be crippled, on crutches, the way George was, and have a mother like Mrs. Gerrold, than to be whole and healthy and have to settle for Annabelle.

"George brought me down to see the dam they're building, and we were about to climb back up the hill when I heard Laurie hurtling through the brush as if the devil himself were after her. Are you going to be able to walk, dear, or shall I help your mother get you out of here?"

"I'm sure we'll manage," Annabelle said at once, regaining her crispness even though her chest was still heaving. "Thank you very much."

Mrs. Gerrold sent another glance in Laurie's direction, then nodded. "Of course. We'll get out of your way, then."

It was an absurd statement, really. There was no reason for them to get out of anyone's way. But Annabelle had already forgotten them. She put down a hand to pull Laurie up. "Come on. You can stand up, can't you? Look what you've done to your clothes!"

Laurie backed away from the outstretched hand and stood up under her own power. She was badly shaken, but not seriously hurt. What would be more painful than anything, she thought, was to have to touch Annabelle. The very thought made her sick to her stomach.

The Gerrolds were making their way up to the backyard of the duplex. Laurie saw that George looked back, but when his mother touched his shoulder he turned away, thrusting himself upward with the aid of the crutches.

Annabelle spoke in a tone low enough that it didn't carry more than a few yards. "Well, that was a foolish thing to do. You might have broken your neck."

Even Laurie was surprised at the words that were forced from between her lips. "Isn't that what you wanted to happen to me?"

Annabelle went pale. "No, of course not. It's stupid to be so upset over a chance remark. I didn't really mean I'd kill you. Everybody says things like that when they're angry, and you'd just broken another of my good plates, and I have this vicious headache . . ."

They stared at one another, both breathing audibly, and for once it was Laurie who was hostile, Annabelle who was placating.

"It was just the sort of thing I say when my head hurts," Annabelle said, and for the first time Laurie saw apprehension in her mother's eyes, perhaps a fear that she had gone too far. "For pete's sake, don't go telling anyone your mother said she'd like to kill you! You'll only be a laughingstock, if they think you took it seriously!"

Laurie was used to making no response to most of what Annabelle said to her, since so often a reply only made her mother more angry. But again she was aware of something new: this time, Annabelle wanted her to talk. This time Annabelle wanted her to say, "All right. I won't tell anyone what you said."

It would have been easy to say, once she got past the lump in her throat. Easy to say, and then probably the worried look would fade out of Annabelle's eyes, and, for the moment, she wouldn't be angry any more.

But Laurie didn't say it. She was trembling, her legs threatening to crumple under her, but she didn't intend to let it show. She stared for a moment more into Annabelle's face, and then she turned away and began to climb the steep bank.

Annabelle followed at a slower pace, making no further attempt to communicate. Laurie didn't know what she was thinking, what she was planning. She only knew that she was afraid of her mother as she never had been before; and her mind worked frantically, if fruitlessly, in an effort to find a way out of her predicament.

She hadn't completely finished the dishes, but Laurie walked right past the sink and up the stairs and into her room. She even pushed the button that locked her bedroom door.

She lay on her bed and watched the twilight come, and then the darkness. Across the hall she could hear Shelly singing to her dolls, and she smelled the glue smell that meant Tim was working on a model.

From Annabelle, there was no sound at all.

She didn't feel like reading, but finally she began to stir and to think that she had to do something. She couldn't just sit forever. As the pain in her twisted wrist faded, a new story began to take place in her mind.

This one wasn't about her father coming and rescuing her, or about being adopted by a rich and beautiful couple who would provide her with dozens of luxuries, nor even about how it would be when she was grown-up and could move away and have a job and a place of her own to live.

This time it was about Annabelle. She pretended that Annabelle was in a horrible accident . . . perhaps she fell down the stairs, as she had on several occasions claimed that Laurie had done . . . and that she was crippled and in a wheelchair. And she pleaded with Laurie and Tim and Shelly to wait on her, to take care of her, to do the things she could no longer do for herself. And maybe she wouldn't even be pretty any more, and Jack would decide that he didn't want a wife who was scarred and couldn't walk, and he'd leave her . . .

No, Laurie thought. No, that would leave Annabelle alone with Laurie, and she didn't want that.

No, Jack would remain devoted to his poor crippled wife, but he'd have to give up his traveling job to take care of her, and maybe that would mean there would be less money, so they'd have to move to a smaller place. And since there wouldn't be enough space, they'd have to find another place for Laurie to live.

She was just trying to figure out where that would be when Tim rapped on her door.

"I'm going to make a sandwich, Laurie. You want one?"

She roused and went to the door. "I don't think I'm hungry."

Tim peered into the room. "What are you doing, sitting here in the dark?"

"Just thinking." Thinking what were probably very wicked thoughts, she decided suddenly, but she didn't care. Even if Annabelle's head did hurt, that wasn't a good enough excuse for saying what she'd said. She *did* hate Laurie, and when she struck out at her, she *did* want to kill her.

"I think there's enough of that homemade bread left for two sandwiches. I'll make you one, too, and if you really don't want it after you see it, I'll help you eat it," Tim decided. Then he looked closer into her face, visible in the hall light. "What's the matter? What happened? Did . . . did she hurt you again? I heard her yelling at you, outside."

"She said," Laurie told him with cold deliberation, "that she'd like to kill me."

Tim's small dark face twisted in protest. "That's a heck of a thing to say to anybody! Listen, Laurie, if you don't want to tell Dad, maybe you could talk to Gram. I think she'd listen to you. I don't think she likes Annabelle very well, anyway."

"What would I tell her?"

"What Annabelle said!"

"She'd deny it. Or she'd laugh and say it was only because I made her mad when she had a headache, and she didn't mean it. She said everybody says things like that when they're angry or they don't feel good."

"Not mothers," Tim argued. "My mother never said anything like that to me or Shelly! She spanked us sometimes, but she never said she'd like to kill us, not even the time I painted the front door with tar!"

"You never talked about your own mother before," Laurie said, for a moment forgetting her own problems. "What was she like?"

"She was nice," Tim said promptly. "She always smelled good, and she baked gingerbread men for us, and she helped me with my models when I was little and couldn't do them alone. She used to sing a lot, and play the piano, and we'd all sing together, even Dad. She laughed a lot, too, until she got sick; but even then she wasn't mean to us, not ever. We really missed her when she went in the hospital. We got to see her a few times, but we weren't supposed to go in there, so for a long time we didn't see her very often. And then she died."

He paused, lifting a bare foot to scratch his other leg. "She wasn't anything like Annabelle."

"It doesn't seem right," Laurie observed, "that someone like your mother should die . . . and someone like Annabelle should be so healthy. All she ever gets are headaches."

Tim nodded. "It's funny Dad married her, isn't it? She's pretty, but that's not important, like being nice. I don't know if my mother was pretty or not, but she sure was nice. You know, I have trouble remembering what she looked like, sometimes. When I dream about her, she's there just the way I remember her. But when I'm awake, it's sort of scary, the way I'm not sure what she looked like."

"You'll always remember what she was really like, how nice she was," Laurie said, and Tim nodded.

"Yeah. Well, I'll bring you a sandwich, too. Be back in a minute."

After he'd gone, Laurie turned on the light and stood looking at herself in the mirror. What was there about her that so infuriated Annabelle? Granted, she looked *something* like her father (she had a small snapshot of him, and she could tell their mouths were sort of the same), but she was a girl and he was a man, and there wasn't all that much the same about them.

What had he done, besides leaving them, to make Annabelle hate him so much that she'd even hate someone who only resembled him?

Tim came back with the sandwich. He'd sliced the bread rather unevenly, so that it was thicker on one end than the other, but that was all right. It was spread with butter and peanut butter that oozed out of the sides; he licked off his own as he handed the other to Laurie.

"I talked to that George kid," he said. "He wants us to go down to the creek early in the morning and work on the dam, and I told him we would. OK?"

"OK," Laurie agreed.

When he had gone, she chewed on the sandwich, surprised at how welcome it was, and again pushed the button that locked her door. She knew it was one of those locks that could be opened by pushing a pin in the hole on the other side, but still it gave her a feeling of being on her own that she liked.

She ate the sandwich very slowly while thumbing through the big dictionary, being careful not to let the peanut butter drip onto it. And then she got ready for bed without going back downstairs to the bathroom for a bath. There was only a little lavatory on the top floor, and she had to wash at the sink. But that was better than taking a chance on seeing Annabelle again tonight.

She was up very early in the morning. She met Tim in the kitchen, and they ate cornflakes and orange juice without talking, so as not to disturb Annabelle, and then they slipped out of the house into the warm summer day.

They were early, but George was there ahead of them, waiting in the shade of the trees at the top of the bank.

They worked all morning, hauling rocks and stout branches for the dam. George couldn't help too much with lifting or dragging anything, but he knew more than either Laurie or Tim about constructing a dam. When he put aside his crutches and sat on the ground, he was able to do most of the actual fitting together of all the materials.

The dam grew, and the sun climbed higher, and they got hotter and dirtier. Somewhere along the line Laurie realized how completely she had thrown herself into the project, how completely she had forgotten everything but the work they were doing, and how contented she felt. Later she would have to go home, and all the problems were still there, but for the time she was happy to be there with George and Tim.

"It's going to be a good pond," George said at last, as they stood watching the water deepen behind the dam. "I'll bet you could even swim in it."

It didn't look to Laurie as if it would be quite deep enough for that, but she was pleased, anyway. She stooped to wash her hands in the pool. "I wish we'd packed a lunch. We could have had a picnic right here, and by the time we finished we could go wading."

"Maybe we could do it yet," Tim said. "If Annabelle isn't around, we could make some sandwiches and take some fruit."

They looked at each other, and Laurie realized that Tim felt just as she did. This had been a special time, a fun time, and if they went to the house and Annabelle scolded them, it would spoil everything.

None of them had watches. George glanced up through the trees. "It must be about eleven o'clock, judging by the sun, wouldn't you say? I bet my mom would fix us a lunch. You want me to go and ask?"

Tim shifted his weight uncomfortably, and Laurie knew again what he was thinking. It didn't seem reasonable to expect someone on crutches to be the one to climb up the bank and look for lunch. "Well, maybe we better go up. Annabelle might be mad if she fixes lunch and there's nobody but Shelly to eat it. Then if she doesn't care, we can fix something ourselves and bring it back down."

So they all went up. Laurie was tired, but it was a good feeling, one of having used her muscles and done something worthwhile. Even if they didn't stay here long enough to enjoy the dam and the pond, it would be there for someone else to use.

The kitchen was empty, the breakfast dishes cleared away and no sign of anything being prepared for lunch. Tim stuck his head through the doorway into the living room where Shelly was working a jigsaw puzzle on the card table.

"Where's Annabelle?"

"She's gone to the mailbox. She's mad at Laurie," Shelly said in the self-righteous manner of one who is still in favor.

"What for?" Tim surveyed his sister with a scowl.

"Because she wasn't here, and Annabelle wanted her to mail an important letter." Shelly placed a piece in the puzzle with an air of triumph.

"Why didn't she just stick in it the mailbox the way she usually does?"

"It was *important*," Shelly said. "The mailman already came, so she had to walk down to the corner box, because it had to go out *today*. She didn't know where you all were. Where were you?"

"Out," Tim said.

Laurie listened to Shelly and Tim, but didn't follow Tim. There was a chance that if she hurried she could fix the sandwiches before Annabelle got back. Even if she was really mad later, it would be worth it to be able to continue the day that had begun so beautifully. She spread mayonnaise on the bread and then mustard, for Tim, and slapped lunch meat and cheese on.

She was reaching for the fruit bowl when she heard it: the screech of brakes, a scream, and then the roar of a motor as a car sped past the front of the house.

Tim was the first to reach the door, but he stopped on the front porch, looking out into the street.

Laurie was only steps behind him, the bag of

sandwiches still clutched in her hand. "What happened? Was there an accident?"

Mrs. Gerrold had come out onto her own porch, and George was behind her, his crutches loud on the wooden steps as they started down.

Tim turned, his face gone suddenly pale.

"It's Annabelle. Laurie, the car hit Annabelle."

Laurie found herself unable to move. She stood there, supported by a hand on the corner post of the porch, staring at the crumpled form in the street.

People were coming from every direction, out of all the houses. It was Saturday, so even some of the men were home, and one of them from directly across the street said, "I'll call the police and an ambulance," and vanished back into his house.

"Did anybody get the license number?"

"Is she dead?"

"Get back, give her some air!"

Laurie and Tim stood where they were as the crowd gathered, enough of them to block Annabelle from their view. Laurie could hear Tim's ragged breathing and her own chest felt paralyzed.

She had made up a story about Annabelle . . . no, more than that, she'd wished it would happen, that Annabelle would have an accident and break her neck. And now . . . she hadn't fallen down the stairs, but she was lying in the street, not moving, and Laurie felt as if she herself were responsible for it.

SEVEN

SHE COULD NOT HONESTLY HAVE
said, then or later, how she felt about Annabelle being hurt. She was frozen in an icy cocoon
that seemed to insulate her from what was happening. She heard the sirens coming, watched the crowd
move back when the police arrived and the officer
knelt beside Annabelle, was aware of the ambulance
and the men putting her mother on a bed with legs
that folded up when it was loaded into the back
of the vehicle, and she felt nothing.

It was Mrs. Gerrold who talked to the police
officers. She nodded toward the three of them on
the porch, where Laurie stood motionless and Tim

held Shelly back with one hand.

"Her name's Summers. These are her children. I don't think her husband is home, is he, Laurie?"

"He's gone to Atlanta, I think," Tim answered, when Laurie could not find her voice.

The policeman asked questions and wrote down the answers in his book, about where Jack worked and when they expected him home and so on.

"Do you know of any relatives who could take care of the kids?" he asked at last.

Mrs. Gerrold turned to them again. "Is there anyone we should call? While we're waiting for the police to reach your father?"

"I'll see if I can get Gram," Tim volunteered, and it wasn't until he'd tried and failed that Mrs. Gerrold spoke again.

"I'll look after them, officer, until their father gets here. We're all living in the same duplex. I'll keep an eye on them, and Laurie's a responsible girl. They'll be all right."

Laurie watched the ambulance drive away, and she wanted to ask if Annabelle was alive or dead, but her lips refused to form the words. Tim didn't ask, either.

It wasn't until everyone had gone away and they were alone that Shelly asked, "Did Annabelle die?"

"We don't know." Tim shot an anxious glance at Laurie. "Are you OK, Laurie?"

She drew a long, shuddering breath. "Yes. I guess there's nothing to do but wait until your father comes home; he'll be able to find out."

So they didn't go back down into the ravine. The beautiful day was spoiled, and yet in a way not completely so, because gradually Laurie lost the numbness and began to think again.

If Annabelle had been killed, what would happen? She, Laurie, wasn't really Jack's responsibility; she was only his stepdaughter. So maybe he wouldn't want her to stay with Tim and Shelly, whatever happened to them. Maybe they'd go and stay with Nell; although when their own mother had died, they'd had a housekeeper who lived-in.

Maybe they'd put Laurie in a foster home. If that happened, would it be a family who would like her? Or would they treat her the same way Annabelle had?

If Annabelle didn't come home, would the police try to find her own father? And if they found him, would he want her? Or was Annabelle right about that, that he didn't care about her and wouldn't want her?

She felt guilty, because she'd wanted something to happen to Annabelle. But there wasn't any way she could have *made* this happen; there was no way she could have controlled any of it, no way she could have kept it from happening. And she didn't honestly know if she would have stopped it if she could have.

Because if Annabelle didn't come home again, Laurie would be free from all her worst fears. Oh, she knew there would be other things to be afraid of, sometimes. Like going to live with strangers and starting over in a new school, things like that.

But she wouldn't have to be afraid that one day her mother's fury would mean that Laurie would be the one taken away in an ambulance to never come home again.

I won't feel guilty, she thought. She hated me, and I was afraid of her, and if she's gone, I won't even feel sorry about it, because she won't ever be able to hurt me again.

Shelly was looking up at her with wide blue eyes. "Laurie . . ."

"Yes, what?"

"If you'd been here, Annabelle would have sent you to the mailbox, wouldn't she? Then would you have got hit by a car?"

For a moment the chill returned. "I don't know. I'd have looked before I crossed the street, I know that. Look, I made some sandwiches. Do you kids want something to eat? It'll probably be a long time before the police get hold of your father, and it'll take him hours to get home. So you might as well have lunch."

Tim and Shelly ate, but Laurie didn't want anything. She cleaned up after they were finished, washed out their glasses and wiped the crumbs off the table. Tim went upstairs to work on his models, and Shelly fell asleep on the sofa in the living room.

Laurie walked restlessly through the house. She

wanted to go down into the ravine, where it was quiet and peaceful, but she didn't dare. She had to be at home in case the telephone rang, in case there was some news about Annabelle, some word from Jack.

At dinnertime Mrs. Gerrold insisted they come over and eat at her house. They'd leave the back doors open so they'd hear the phone if it rang, she said.

So they went, and Laurie never remembered what they ate. But she did absorb the atmosphere there, of a normal family who enjoyed one another's company. George's father was a big, red-headed man with ears just like George's, and Laurie thought if he hadn't been concerned about them because of what happened to Annabelle, he'd have laughed and talked a lot more than he did.

If she went to a foster family, might they be something like the Gerrolds? she wondered.

It was nearly Shelly's bedtime, and Laurie had just got her into the tub, when Jack came home.

They heard his step on the porch, then his key in the lock, and they turned expectantly toward the front door.

"Hi, kids. You all OK?" he asked. Shelly had climbed out of the tub and stood, dripping, on the carpet. "Hey, jellybean, you'd better get back in the bathroom before you drown us all," he said, but he didn't sound the same as usual.

Laurie licked her lips. "Have . . . have you seen? . . ."

"Annabelle? Yeah, I just came from the hospital. She's pretty well banged up, and she has a broken collarbone and a concussion, but she's going to be all right. She'll be home in a few days, maybe. Until then, I'll take time off, or maybe I can get Ma to come and stay with you. Come on, now, Shelly, back in the tub. Looks like Laurie's been managing all right." He sent Laurie a look of approval and followed Shelly into the bathroom.

Tim looked at Laurie. "She didn't die."

"No."

"She'll be home in a few days, he said."

"Yes." There was a sharp, painful ache in her throat. She didn't actually *wish* that Annabelle had died. But the thought that her mother was coming home, that it would all go on as before, brought Laurie to the point of tears, and she turned away to hide them.

As it turned out, Annabelle didn't come home for a week, and it was one of the best times Laurie could remember. The first three days only Jack was there with them, and he didn't care what they did or where they did it. Then Nell came, just to do the cooking and the laundry, she said, because Laurie and Tim could handle things nicely, only Shelly couldn't be left alone while they were in school.

Laurie kept trying to bring herself to talk to someone, some adult who might help her, because she dreaded the time when Annabelle would come home. Only every teacher she thought of had to be rejected for one reason or another. Most of them just seemed too busy, and they didn't really seem to care about kids' problems; she supposed they had problems of their own.

She thought about telling the school nurse, and she even went to her office several times, but finally gave up. There was simply no way to get the nurse alone long enough to discuss anything in private. And the second time Laurie was there, the nurse sort of frowned at her and said, "What, are you here again?" in an impatient way.

She considered trying to talk to Nell, too, but she couldn't quite bring herself to do that, either. Nell seemed different when she was around all the time, busy with things.

The best part of the week was the time she spent, after school, with George.

Every day he was waiting for her when she got home, and they went down into the ravine. Once Tim went with them, and they each made a fleet of boats out of leaves and had battles on the pond. But the rest of the time it was only Laurie and George. Sometimes they pretended various things, and sometimes they just sat on the creek bank and told each other stories from books they'd read.

And then, the last day, the day before Annabelle was to come home, George met her just as before, but he was grinning slyly.

"You'll never guess what I found today," he offered.

"Probably not," Laurie agreed. She was trying not

to think about her mother (would Annabelle feel it was *her* fault she'd been hit by a car, because it should have been Laurie who went to the mailbox?), and she was determined to enjoy her freedom while she had it.

"I've hidden it down in the woods. Come and see," George said. "It's a secret, even from Tim, OK?"

"OK," Laurie agreed. She tried to sound casual, but she was beginning to get excited. She'd never had a friend to share secrets with before, and maybe it was something worthwhile.

George led the way over the bank and down the hill, but not toward the dam. Instead, he angled away from the back of the duplex, into an area Laurie hadn't explored.

Suddenly he stopped, listening, and Laurie listened, too.

At first all she heard was some silly bird, singing his little heart out as if all were right with the world, and the gurgle of the creek below. And then she heard another sound that brought her eyes around to George's face.

"It's over there. Behind that big tree." George flung aside his crutches and dropped to the ground, leaning forward toward something she couldn't see. Laurie moved up beside him and stopped.

There in a hollow between the tree roots was a puppy.

Laurie drew in her breath in awe. He was a rich,

116

golden brown, with long silky ears and enormous sad eyes, and he yelped when he saw them, and wagged his stumpy tail without trying to stand up.

"I think somebody dumped him off this morning," George said. "I heard a car stop, and I looked out and saw him in the street, and the car took off, real fast, and then another car came along and this poor little guy didn't get out of the way fast enough. He got hit, and for a few minutes he just laid there, and I thought he was dead."

Just like Annabelle, Laurie thought. She knelt beside George and put out a hand to stroke the animal's head. It was marvelously warm and soft, and the puppy twisted to lick at her fingers.

"I don't know if he's got a broken leg or not, but he won't stand on that back one," George said. "I know you know something about broken bones. Maybe you can tell."

Laurie felt a rush of warmth and compassion as she carefully maneuvered the puppy to explore the injured leg. He whimpered, but licked again at her hand, as if he knew that she didn't mean to hurt him.

"I guess he's a golden retriever," George said. "At least, he looks a lot like the picture of golden retriever puppies I've got in a book."

"I don't know for sure about his leg," Laurie said soberly. "I don't feel any place where the bones are out of place. One time I had a broken wrist, and you could feel the lump where the bones came apart and one end sort of slid up over the top of the other one. But a bone can be fractured without the ends coming apart. If it is, you put a splint on it until it heals."

"And that takes quite a while," George observed, putting his own hand out to be licked .

"Probably about six weeks," Laurie confirmed. "What are you going to do with him?"

"Well, there's a rule against dogs here, so I can't very well take him in the house and keep him there. My folks like dogs, but they won't break the rules. I wondered if we couldn't just keep him down here, make him a house and feed him without anybody's knowing about it. He's little; he won't eat much."

Laurie withdrew and sat down, crosslegged, to review the situation. At that, the puppy staggered to his feet, and on three legs made his way to her.

"Look, he can walk! Maybe he'll just not walk on that one leg until it gets better. I think he likes me."

When she bent over, an enthusiastic pink tongue lapped at her face, making her laugh. George was grinning, too.

"What do you think, Laurie? Will you help me take care of him and keep him hidden down here?"

"We'll have to teach him not to bark, or someone will find him."

"And give him a name. He needs a name."

They stared at one another, both smiling, and then they shook hands on it. They would keep the dog, and he would be their own private secret.

They built him a house out of cardboard boxes and camouflaged it with branches and leaves. George found a length of clothesline to secure the pup to a tree, giving him enough leeway to reach the creek for water. Laurie brought an old plastic container that had had cottage cheese in it, filled now with bread crumbled into lukewarm soup, for his first meal. The puppy gulped eagerly, the floppy ears hanging out on each side of the cheese carton.

They decided to call him *Amigo*, which meant *friend* in Spanish. George had just read a book that had a lot of Spanish words in it.

"It may be tricky, getting food out to him, once *she* comes home," Laurie said thoughtfully.

"We can get him some puppy food. I'll pay for it out of my allowance," George said. "And maybe by the time he needs more than I can afford, we'll be moving back home, and he can go live in the country."

Annabelle came home the next afternoon. Laurie felt even more upset waiting than she had expected to be. Would Annabelle blame her for what had happened?

But when Jack brought her home, Annabelle scarcely looked at her at all. She said she was so tired she wanted to go right to bed.

She looked strange, with bruises turning greenish-yellow on her face and arms, and a row of black sutures remaining in the hairline at one temple. She was supposed to go to the doctor's office the next day to have them taken out.

She looked, Laurie thought, like something out of a Frankenstein movie. Not beautiful at all.

Her left arm was in a sling, secured against her chest in such a way that she wouldn't hurt her collarbone before it healed. She walked unsteadily and Jack had to hold her up. It was a relief to Laurie when she vanished into her bedroom and closed the door.

"You kids play outside and keep it quiet so she can rest, OK?" Jack suggested when he came out. "She isn't going to do much for a while, and you'll have to pitch in."

Laurie would have gladly taken on the whole house if it had meant Annabelle would stay out of sight, but of course she knew that wasn't going to happen.

But during the days that Annabelle stayed pretty much in her room, Laurie continued to enjoy her new-found freedom. Nobody asked where she was, all that mattered was that no one disturbed Annabelle. So Laurie spent most of her time down in the ravine with George and Amigo.

In only a short time Amigo came to know his name. He also learned not to bark when they went away and left him; for when he barked, George would slap him with a rolled-up newspaper. They hated to do it, he was such an affectionate little creature, but it was for his own good. He must not make his presence known to anyone else.

Amigo recovered from his injury faster than Annabelle did from hers. Within a week he was walking on all four legs, climbing up on whoever got close to him first.

Annabelle, however, continued to move slowly, to spend long hours lying on the couch reading or watching television, and even after Nell went home (she had been coming over during the day so that Annabelle didn't have to watch over Shelly by herself), she didn't get up to do anything in the kitchen. Jack cooked if he were home; the rest of the time, Laurie and Tim managed.

School was finally out for the summer, and Laurie looked forward to Annabelle remaining an invalid for a long time, and to spending her days down by the creek with George and Amigo. Tim knew there was something up between them, but he didn't press when Laurie explained she'd promised to keep it a secret. Tim had met a group of boys who played ball over in the playground, and he spent most of his time with them, so Laurie didn't feel really guilty about the secret.

And then one day George didn't meet her in the ravine, and when she knocked timidly on his back door, no one answered. She spent the day reading and playing with Amigo, and when she went up to the house late in the afternoon to start dinner, the Gerrolds were still gone.

The following morning, after she'd soft boiled an

egg and made toast to Annabelle's exacting standards, Laurie closed the screened door quietly behind her and listened to the sounds coming from the adjoining apartment. Someone was home, now. But she was afraid Annabelle would hear her if she knocked and asked for George.

She knew, though, when she started down into the ravine, that George was ahead of her. She could see the marks from his crutches in the soft earth.

She made her way down the bank and found her friends, not at the house they'd made for Amigo, but at the dam. Amigo trotted toward her, tail wagging happily, and George turned, too.

"Hey, you know there's a fish in our pond?"

"No, is there? What kind?"

She stood beside him and watched the silvery minnow investigating the dam, as if it were looking for a way out of its prison.

"I don't know what kind. Maybe he'll get big enough so we can fish for him."

"I don't think I want to catch him," Laurie said after a moment.

"No. I guess I don't, either." George sat down on a warm rock, crutches leaning beside him, and put down a hand to fondle Amigo's silky ears. "Anyway, it would be a long time before he was big enough to bother with."

There was something odd about the way he spoke, and Laurie turned to face him. "I missed you yesterday," she said softly.

George cleared his throat. "Yeah. I didn't get

down here all day." There was a silence, and then he added, "I was at the hospital. I had to have some tests."

Suddenly Laurie felt the tremor that she sometimes got in her legs when she knew something bad was going to happen. "Is . . . is everything all right?" she asked, and even before he answered, she knew it wasn't.

"Well . . . I've got to go back in and have another operation."

At their feet the water burbled over the top of the dam, and Amigo made soft whimpering noises to get their attention. Overhead the leaves were a cool green, keeping off most of the sun, and they made rustling sounds. Laurie thought of the good times they'd had here the past month, she and George, and she knew that she didn't want them to end.

The fun with George and Amigo was all that made life bearable for her.

Her throat ached when she spoke. "Will you have to be there very long?"

George didn't look at her, and she knew their good times meant a lot to him, too. "I usually stay in about two months, every time they operate. Maybe it won't be so long this time, though."

Two months! Practically the whole summer, when she had looked forward to spending her vacation with him!

He did look at her then. "You'll have to take care of Amigo."

"Yes. Until you get back."

George plucked at a few blades of grass growing in a crack in the rock. "Maybe . . . maybe he'll forget me, while I'm gone. If he does, he'd better . . . he'd better be *your* dog, Laurie."

And that was all they said about it. He didn't have to check into the hospital until the next Monday, and they continued to meet and to talk and to play with Amigo as if that were all they would be doing all summer.

Only at night, when she was alone, did Laurie think of how much she'd miss George when he went away. She couldn't even be sure they'd still be here when he got back, although Annabelle hadn't said anything about moving again.

She wanted to give him something for a going away present, but she didn't have any money. So at the last minute, she snatched up her shell, the lovely pink one Jack had brought her, and thrust it into his hand just as he and his mother were getting into their car to go.

George looked at it and grinned. "Hey, thanks, Laurie. It's a real neat shell. Maybe I'll start a shell collection."

And then he was gone, and Laurie blinked hard against the stinging in her eyes and watched until the car was out of sight. George was the first real friend she'd ever had, and she wondered if she'd ever see him again.

EIGHT

T HE LONELINESS SHE'D KNOWN almost all her life was nothing compared to
what she felt the first few days after George went
away. Mrs. Gerrold saw her sitting on the back
steps and came over to talk to her on Tuesday afternoon; she looked tired and as if she'd been under a
strain.

"The operation seemed to go all right. George was
coming out from under the anesthetic just before I
left, and he sent you a rather cryptic message. At
least I didn't understand it. He said, 'Tell Laurie to
be sure to take care of Amigo.' Does that mean
anything to you?"

"Yes," Laurie said with a small, sad smile. "It's a secret, though. I can't tell you." It meant, she thought, that George was thinking about her the same as she was thinking about him.

Mrs. Gerrold nodded. "Well, we hope this may be the last operation he has to have, at least for a few years. Maybe we can take him home to our own house when he gets out of the hospital this time."

So he wouldn't be returning even if Annabelle didn't make them move again!

Laurie sat for a long time after Mrs. Gerrold had gone in, wondering why life had to be so painful. She didn't think it was always that way for everybody. Girls she had known at school seemed to be happy most of the time, to have friends and parents who cared about them. Even George, for all his difficulties, had parents who really cared.

"Laurie? What are you sitting there mooning about?"

She lifted her head and looked at Annabelle, in the doorway. "I was just . . . thinking."

"About what?"

Resentment stirred inside her. Why should she have to tell anyone what she was thinking? Thoughts were private, and nobody, not even a parent, should be able to demand to know what they were.

She hadn't replied, and Annabelle's mouth flattened in a familiar way. "Your father used to do the same thing. Just sit and ignore me when I asked him a question, as if he couldn't care less what I was talking about. He didn't even have the common courtesy to acknowledge the fact that I was speaking to him. You get more like him every day . . . sullen and uncooperative."

How could she reply to a statement like that? Laurie wondered. She couldn't think of anything to say, so she sat still, wrapped in her own unhappiness.

Annabelle's mouth twisted in an ugly grimace. "I thought that woman said something about a message from George."

Laurie swallowed. "Yes. He just had his operation today. He . . . he was thinking about me, is all."

"She said something about taking care of Amigo. What did that mean?"

Fright sent a fine tremor through her, and she hoped Annabelle didn't notice it. "He was just coming out from under the anesthetic. He was probably dreaming something, the way people do then."

For a moment Annabelle didn't move, and then she turned abruptly and went back into the house without speaking.

She doesn't believe me, Laurie thought. She knows George and I have a secret, and she won't rest until she knows what it is.

She couldn't think of anything she could do with Amigo to hide him more safely, except to take him further away, up the other side of the ravine. And if she did that, tied him away from the stream, she'd have to carry water to him regularly.

He was such a clumsy thing that he'd probably overturn any water dish she put out for him. And what if there was a day when she couldn't get to him? A day when Annabelle kept her so busy she couldn't slip out, or even a day when Annabelle had hurt her so that she couldn't take care of the dog?

Amigo was only a puppy. He needed plenty of fresh water and food several times a day. If he weren't taken care of, he'd probably cry and bark and people would hear him. The more she thought about it, the worse it all seemed, until she came to the only possible conclusion.

She'd have to share the secret with Tim, so that he could help her.

She waited until they'd all gone up to bed that evening. Annabelle didn't bother to try to get up and down stairs; she saw to it that Shelly took her bath, and then let her go up to bed by herself. Laurie busied herself with her big dictionary for a while, looking up some marvelous words like "rictus," which meant the gaping of a mouth, especially that of a bird, and "sculpin," which was a variety of big-headed, spiny fish.

When, at last, the house grew quiet, except for the sound of the television far away downstairs, Laurie moved quietly across the landing and tapped on Tim's door.

"Tim? Can I come in?"

"Sure." He was in his pajamas, sprawled across his

bed looking through a model catalog. "Hi. Boy, have I found a neat model. I'm going to tell Dad it's what I want when my birthday comes."

He rolled over so that Laurie could sit on the foot of the bed, where she drew up her knees under her chin.

"Something wrong?" he wanted to know.

"Well, sort of. Tim, I had a secret with George. And now he's going to be in the hospital for two months, and maybe when he comes out he won't even come back here to live, his mother said. They might go home to their place in the country. So I have to tell somebody else . . . about the secret, I mean."

Tim forgot the catalog and sat crosslegged, facing her. "OK. You can tell me, Laurie. I'll keep it a secret."

"I'm telling you because I need some help," she said, and Tim nodded expectantly. "George found this dog, you see. Well, he's only a puppy, really. He got hurt but now he's all right, he can walk and everything. Only there's a rule against pets here, so he didn't dare take Amigo home with him. And now George is gone, and I'll have to take care of him, and I'm afraid Annabelle is suspicious. Amigo, that's his name, he's hidden down in the ravine. But she knows I spend a lot of time down there, and if she goes looking, she could find him. George bought his some dog food, but if I move him away from the creek, I'll have to check a couple of times a day to see if Amigo has water, and some days that may be hard to do."

Tim's mouth curved in a slow grin. "A dog! Hey, that's neat! What kind is he?"

"George thinks he's a golden retriever. Anyway, he's this golden color, and he's so soft and silky and friendly . . . I can't let anything happen to him, Tim."

Tim's grin widened. "Amigo, huh?"

"That means *friend* in Spanish."

"Amigo. That's a good name for a dog." His grin faded abruptly. "You're right. If Annabelle is suspicious, we better find a good place to hide him. Tell you what, let's go down first thing in the morning and take a look at him. Then we'll decide what to do."

"We don't want to make it too obvious where we're going all the time. Annabelle might follow us."

"Yeah. But she's used to you going down there a lot, anyway. Don't worry, Laurie, I'll help you take care of him," Tim assured her. He seemed so sure, that Laurie began to feel sure herself that Amigo would be all right.

Amigo was only too happy to have a new friend. He and Tim hit it off at once. Together, Laurie and Tim took apart the doghouse, which was already growing too small for Amigo anyway, and then put the parts together to make a larger home for him, far up on the other side of the ravine.

At first, when they started to go off and leave him in the new place, Amigo objected to being left there. He barked.

"No," Laurie told him sternly. "You can't bark, or she'll hear you, and then you're done for."

"How did you keep him from barking before?" Tim wanted to know.

"George spanked him with a newspaper. But we haven't got one here now."

"There's a branch I can use for a switch. Maybe that'll work. You go first, Laurie, since it's you that's his best friend. And then wait on top of the hill. If I can't make him be quiet when I leave, and you hear him bark, get a newspaper and bring it back."

So they tried that, and after Tim had swatted him twice with the branch, Amigo crept sadly into his house and watched with mournful eyes as the two of them disappeared into the woods.

For several days everything went easily. They managed to keep Amigo watered and fed, between them, even though Annabelle expected both of them to do a lot of chores around the house.

Annabelle had had her stitches out, but one side of her face was still swollen and showed traces of the bruises that had discolored it. She seemed short-tempered with all of them, even Shelly, sometimes even when Jack was around. He would simply tell them to go off and play somewhere else, and he never had to suggest it twice. Had Laurie and Tim had their way, they would never have come near Annabelle at all.

But Jack wasn't home most of the time, of course. He went off for almost a week to Detroit. Then they all just stayed away as much as they could, even Shelly. And Annabelle seemed glad to be rid of them, except when she wanted things done.

Lulled almost into a sense of security because Annabelle had been paying no attention to them at all, Laurie and Tim had spent the morning and part of one afternoon down in the ravine. They had allowed Amigo to run loose while they constructed a miniature waterfall out of rocks above the dam, and they shared their sandwiches and fruit with him at lunchtime. They had discovered that Amigo was very fond of both apples and bananas, but would not eat oranges.

They had had a good time, and they were tired and rather dirty when they decided they'd better go up and see if Annabelle wanted them to do something about dinner. Since Jack was coming home that night she might want something from the store. They thought she'd probably cook herself, but she'd complained of a headache earlier so there was nothing certain about that.

Annabelle was lying down with a cold cloth over her eyes. When Laurie asked timidly if she should do something about dinner, her mother spoke crossly. "Do anything you like. Just leave me alone."

Laurie and Tim held a low-voiced consultation

and decided they would make a meatloaf out of hamburger and put it in the oven with potatoes to bake. There would probably be time after Jack got home to fix a salad to go with them.

Until it was time to do that, they both went upstairs, Tim to work on his latest model, Laurie to curl up with a new book.

Neither of them realized anything was wrong until they heard the excited barking from the backyard.

Laurie sprang up in alarm, rushing to her window to look out, but she couldn't see anything. Surely it wasn't Amigo, they'd left him securely tied to a tree on the far side of the ravine . . .

She collided with Tim on the upper landing and saw her own consternation mirrored on his face.

"It sure sounds like him," Tim muttered, and led the dash down the stairs.

It was too late.

Annabelle, still holding the wet washcloth in one hand, stood in the middle of the kitchen staring at the small, yelping animal on the other side of the screened door.

"Stop it! Stop that racket! Go away!" she commanded furiously.

Amigo, of course, did nothing of the sort. He had spotted his friends, and all he wanted was to get to them.

"Get him away from here!" Annabelle cried. Even during the excitement of the moment it struck

Laurie that her mother sounded afraid of the dog, small though he was.

Laurie moved quickly to the door; but the moment she opened it, to go out, Amigo rushed inside. The trailing rope that dangled from his neck told the story: he had chewed through it and followed the familiar scent to the back door of the duplex.

Amigo, unaware of the problems he was causing, waggled his whole behind in joy. Not only were his children here, but he could smell the cooking meatloaf. Surely this was a better place than his lonesome ravine!

Laurie and Tim both snatched at the rope, but couldn't hold on to it. And Amigo made for Annabelle, obviously thinking that here was a new human, a new friend.

Laurie caught a glimpse of her mother's pale face, contorted in what might have been either anger or alarm, and then heard Amigo's yelp of pain when Annabelle kicked out at him. The blow sent him sliding across the floor, but Annabelle wasn't satisfied with that.

She seized the broom that stood beside the door and began to beat the puppy with it. Poor Amigo would have been only too happy at that point to run back to his ravine, but he was cornered.

"No, don't!" Laurie protested, risking being beaten herself to rush in and rescue the dog. She picked him up and started toward the door. "He won't hurt anything, I'll take him out, don't . . ."

The broom crashed down on her shoulder with numbing force, and she heard Tim cry out in protest, and then another blow landed against the side of her head so that there was a ringing sound in her ears.

"Stop it!" Tim was yelling. "Stop it, I'll tell my dad on you! Don't hurt Laurie!"

Laurie kept backing toward the door, feeling as if she were in the midst of some terrible nightmare. But she didn't awaken, and the blows rained down on her head and shoulders while Amigo whimpered pathetically when he, too, was struck.

Dimly, Laurie realized that Annabelle had dropped the broom and was now hitting her with something heavier, something that cut into her arms and hands and made her loosen her hold on the dog; and then, for the first time in her life, she lost consciousness in one brilliant explosion of color and pain.

She was aware of the pain before she opened her eyes. She heard Tim's anxious voice and felt his hand on her arm. "Laurie? Wake up, Laurie, please!"

She opened her eyes reluctantly. She didn't want to wake up, she didn't want Annabelle to hit her anymore . . .

"She's gone," Tim said. His face was streaked with tears, and there was a bluish streak across one cheek where he'd gotten in the way of the broom handle. "She's gone, and I was afraid she'd killed you . . ."

Laurie pushed herself into a sitting position. She hurt all over. "Where's Amigo?"

Tim shook his head, wiping a hand over his running nose. "I don't know. When you fell down, she kept hitting you with the fireplace poker, and I was afraid she was killing you; and when I tried to make her stop, she shoved me in the closet and I couldn't get out. I heard Amigo yip a couple of times, and then I didn't hear anything. I couldn't get out until Shelly came downstairs and opened the door."

Laurie looked past him to see Shelly, her eyes wide and frightened, watching them. "Where's . . . *she*?"

Tim shook his head again. "I don't know. Shelly didn't see her, either. Maybe Amigo got away, maybe he ran back down in the ravine."

They looked at one another, neither of them believing that, much as they wanted to. Laurie got up and went to the sink to wash off the worst of the stinging places. That only made them worse, so she stopped. There was a large tender lump behind one ear, and she didn't touch that.

"We'd better go look for him," she said, and without further words they crossed the backyard and made their way down to the creek, calling for Amigo as they went.

There was no sign of him. His water dish had been overturned, and the severed rope trailed out from the tree where they'd tied him. But Amigo was nowhere to be found.

"Tim," Laurie said at last, when they had to give

up, "I can't do it anymore. I can't live this way."

"Dad'll be home pretty soon. We'll tell him," Tim said. "He's got to do something. She was like she was crazy. He won't let her be that way to us."

Shelly piped up from her position, trudging up the bank a few steps behind them. "He's not coming, Tim."

Tim stopped and stared at his sister almost angrily. "What do you mean, he's not coming? He's supposed to be back tonight."

Shelly shook her head. "No. There was a telephone call, and it made Annabelle's head hurt more. Daddy's flight was cancelled, and he's going to be late."

Tim scowled. "Late? How late?"

But that Shelly didn't know. "What's cancelled, Tim?"

"It means his airplane, the one he was supposed to come home on, didn't take off for some reason."

They reached the backyard and looked across it. They all saw the back door close.

"She's there," Tim said unnecessarily.

Laurie was shaking so that it was all she could do to stand. "I can't go back in there, Tim. I can't. I'm so tired, and I'm scared. . . . She hates me . . ."

"I don't want to live with her anymore, either," Tim agreed. "Well, if Dad's not coming home, we'll just have to run away."

Shelly appeared ready to cry. "Do I have to run away, too?"

"It . . . it's not just running away," Laurie said

unsteadily. "We have to have a place to run *to*. And there isn't any place."

"Oh, yes, there is. We'll go to Gram's. I went there with her once on the bus," Tim said. "I can find it again."

Laurie's hand came up to rub the shoulder where Annabelle had struck her. It ached something awful. What she really wanted to do was to crawl into bed and fall asleep, but she was afraid to go into the house.

"Shall we?" Tim asked. "Go to Gram's? I've got enough of my last allowance left to pay our bus fare."

"Me, too?" Shelly wanted to know.

Laurie released a shuddering sigh. "OK. Let's go to your grandmother's," she said, but she had a terrible feeling that no matter where she went, Annabelle would find her.

NINE

THE BUS FARE TOOK ALL OF TIM'S money except fifteen cents. Shelly was tired before they even reached the bus stop, and she wanted to go back home as soon as the bus came and they got on.

"We can't go home," Tim said fiercely, shaking her by the arm.

"Why?" Shelly asked, her blue eyes filling with tears.

"Because Annabelle's there, and she..." He stopped, his eyes meeting Laurie's. Shelly hadn't seen what happened in the kitchen; she didn't understand why they were running away. And he didn't

want to tell her what Annabelle had done.

Laurie reached down and took Shelly's hand. "It's all right, Shelly. You can rest on the bus. Don't you want to go to your grandma's?"

The bus driver hadn't paid any attention to them at all, though several of the passengers looked at them curiously. But for once Laurie didn't care who stared at her, or why. She was too worried about what was going to happen. Because this was going to be *it*.

If they appealed to Nell, and she didn't believe what they said, Laurie knew she'd never have the courage to try again. Not ever, with anyone else.

If Nell made them go back home to Annabelle . . . but that was too awful to think about. When Annabelle had those spells, she just wasn't sane anymore. Maybe she'd never been sane. Normal mothers didn't do the things Annabelle did, did they?

They huddled together on the bus seat while the bus roared along the street, stopping every couple of blocks to pick up or let off passengers. It seemed to Laurie that the ride went on forever. In a way she wished that it would, because she dreaded having to tell Nell all the terrible things that Annabelle had done. But in another way, she wanted it all over and done with; there was no way to go back, and she wanted to know what was going to happen next.

If Nell didn't believe her . . .

No, she wouldn't think about that. Not yet. Not until she had to. She'd think about. . . . She hadn't really meant to think about Amigo, because that hurt, too.

Only she couldn't help thinking about him because she was afraid that maybe Annabelle had done something to him, or he'd run into the street and been killed by a car. Either way, he might be lying somewhere, hurt, needing help, and she didn't know where to find him. Poor, foolish, little Amigo, who had chewed through his rope in order to follow Laurie home.

"When are we going to get there?" Shelly asked. "I'm hungry."

"Pretty soon," Tim said. He looked over her head at Laurie. "It's a little walk after we get off the bus. We go as far as it goes, and then we have to walk a ways. She lives sort of out in the country, you know."

They were the only ones left on the bus when it came to the end of the line. It wasn't quite country, there were still lots of houses, but no sidewalks. Laurie tried to put down her fears and stay in control of herself, because if there was one thing she couldn't afford, it was to make a bad impression on Nell. Nell was her only hope.

"I'm tired," Shelly said in a whining voice. "I don't want to walk any farther, Tim."

"You have to, or we can't get to Gram's. Come on, we'll pull you."

When they had walked several blocks and the houses were thinning out, Laurie noticed that Tim was peering intently ahead of them. She hoped he wasn't lost.

"Do you see her house yet?"

"No. But it can't be much further. It's a yellow house, and it has a white fence around it."

It was another four blocks, and by the time they reached it, all three were exhausted. Shelly was crying openly as they dragged her along, which probably wasn't going to make a very good impression on Nell, Laurie thought. She hoped Nell wouldn't think they were deliberately being mean to Shelly.

Tim was reaching for the latch on the front gate when a car rolled to a stop beside them and a police officer stuck his head out of the window.

"Well, there, what's the matter?"

Fright drew all the remaining color out of Laurie's cheeks. She gripped Shelly's hand tightly and shook her head. "Nothing. We're just going in there." She gestured at Nell's yellow house.

The officer turned off the ignition and sat looking at them in such a way that they didn't dare keep on going. "The little one acts like something's the matter, all right. What's she crying about?"

"She's tired and hungry," Tim said. He'd opened the gate but didn't go through it.

"Likely she is, this time of day. Suppertime, eh?" The officer got out of the police car. He was very tall and he wore a tan uniform. "What're your names?"

Shelly didn't know whether to go on crying or

not. She looked up at the man suspiciously. "I'm hungry," she told him.

"I'll bet you are. What's your name?"

"Shelly."

"Shelly. What are you really doing, Shelly? Are you running away from home? All three of you? Away from a nice home over on Prospect Street?"

A cold dread filled Laurie's chest, and she felt Shelly's fingers slipping away from hers. Annabelle had called the police!

The officer looked at Laurie then, the tallest of the trio. "You're a big girl to be running off just because you had an argument with your mother, aren't you?"

An argument! Was that what Annabelle had told him? Laurie's throat constricted, and she was unable to speak.

"We're going to see our grandmother. What's wrong with that?" Tim demanded, tugging at Laurie, trying to pull her into the front yard.

"I didn't want to run away," Shelly said. "I was too tired, but they said I had to go, too."

"Well, why don't you all get into the back seat, and I'll give you a ride home? How would that be? Aren't you about ready to go home now and have your supper?"

Shelly made a move toward him, but Tim jerked her back. "No! We came to see Gram, and we're going to see her!" He turned toward the house, pulling his sister protestingly along, yelling at the top of his voice. "Grandma Nell! Gram, Gram!"

"Here, now, just a minute," the officer said, and Laurie thought he was going to take hold of her, since she was the only one within reach. She blurted out the first words that came to her tongue.

"We haven't done anything wrong, you can't arrest us when we didn't do anything wrong . . ."

"I'm not going to arrest anyone. Your mother called the police because she said you'd run away, and she's worried about you. I'll just give you a ride home, and that will be that."

"Gram!" Tim's last shriek finally brought results, for Nell appeared at last on the front porch. She squinted down at them in alarm. "Tim! What on earth's going on?" She came down the steps to meet them, pausing when Tim grabbed her hand, but watching the police officer. "What's the trouble?"

"A trio of runaways," the officer said. "Mrs. Summers called in and said she'd scolded the kids and they got angry and ran away. She thought maybe they'd come here to your house, but she couldn't reach you on the phone, so I came to take a look. I'll just give them a ride on home, and everything will be all taken care of."

Laurie stood frozen, watching Nell's face, anguish written on her own. If he took them back, what would Annabelle do, once she was alone with them?

"Just a minute, officer," Nell said. "I think I'd better know a little more about this. Tim, shush a minute. Let's all go inside where the neighbors won't overhear everything we say and talk about this."

"Runaways, pure and simple, ma'am. I'm due to go home on my supper break in a few minutes, but I'll take the kids home, first."

"No, I don't think so. I'll take the responsibility for them," Nell said slowly. She looked hard at Laurie, then down at Tim who was still tugging at her hand. "I'm their grandmother. I won't let anything happen to them. I'll call their mother and tell her where they are."

"She's not *my* mother," Tim said angrily. "She's my stepmother, and she's hateful and wicked, and when I tell my dad what she did . . ."

"Tim." Nell's hand came down hard on his shoulder. "Wait until we're inside." And then, to the officer, "Said she'd scolded them, did she?"

"That's what she told the dispatcher, yes, ma'am. Scolded them, and they decided to run away."

"But they haven't broken any laws, have they? There's no reason for them to be taken into custody? Why don't you run along and have your dinner, officer, and I'll see to the kids."

"Well, all right, Mrs. Summers, if that's what you want. I'll check in with the dispatcher and let him know. And you'll talk to their mother, right?"

Tim opened his mouth, and Nell put her hand over it. "Inside, kids. Thank you, officer."

They went up the front steps to the house. Laurie was shaking so that she was glad when Nell herded them into the dining room and told them to sit down.

"Now. I made a big pot of soup this afternoon, just the way I used to do when all my family was home, and I'm going to dish up a bowl for each of us. And while we eat, you can tell me what this is all about. Tim, bring a washrag from the bathroom for Shelly's face, and I'll set three more places."

At first Laurie didn't think she could eat anything without having it come right back up. But the soup was hot and delicious, and after the first few spoonsful her stomach felt better.

"Now," Nell said, "I think I'd better hear the whole story."

The whole story was not a simple one. Telling it took a long time. Nell alternated between urging Tim to calm down and prodding gently to get a reply out of Laurie; but after a while they had all finished what they had to say. Laurie sat with her hands in her lap, and they had almost stopped trembling. Almost, but not quite.

"And this has been going on since you were three years old," Nell said at last, quietly, looking at Laurie. "You poor child! And you never told anybody." She sighed. "I suspected something but nothing as bad as this. It's hard to believe . . ."

But Nell did believe it, Laurie thought. She was rather numb, and she still didn't dare to hope, really hope; but it was as if a crack had appeared in the block of ice which encased her. Would Nell try to help her?

There were sudden heavy footsteps on the front

porch, the doorbell rang, and then before anybody could move to answer it, Jack and Annabelle burst through the doorway.

Laurie began to shrivel in her chair.

"Ma? The cops said the kids were here, but you didn't call. For pete's sake, didn't you realize Annabelle was frantic?"

Nell pushed back her chair and stood up. "Was she? Yes, I imagine she was. Well, they were very tired and hungry, and I thought they needed attending to. Maybe you'd both better sit down. We have quite a bit to talk about, I think."

Annabelle's face was flushed, and she didn't have any make-up on. Normally she never left the house without putting on make-up first. Her eyes were very bright, and she looked at Laurie, and then quickly back at Nell.

"I think it's time they were taken home to bed. It's late, nearly Shelly's bedtime, and she looks about ready to fall asleep, right off her chair."

"Jack can put her in on the couch and let her sleep there. I mean it, Jack, this is important. I think you'd better hear what the kids have just told me before you do anything at all."

Jack stared around at their faces, bewildered. "What's going on? Look, Ma, if the kids lipped off to Annabelle, that's a family problem, and Annabelle and I will take care of it."

Nell's voice was very soft, so soft that it was more impressive than if she'd shouted. "It's a bigger family problem than you think, Jack. Big enough so

148

we'd all better sit down and talk about it."

Annabelle's eyes were snapping dangerously. "Come on, Laurie. Go get in the car. Jack, if you carry Shelly, Tim can open the door for you . . ."

Nell rested a hand on Laurie's shoulder, warm and reassuring, except that Laurie was too terrified to believe in the message. "No, Annabelle. Laurie isn't going anywhere, not yet. Not if I have to call the police back in order to keep you from taking her home."

Now it was Jack's face that began to get red. He swore, but more as if he were astounded at his mother's attitude than because he was angry with her. "Now, look, Ma, she's Annabelle's kid . . . you've got no right to interfere where Laurie is concerned."

"When you hear what Laurie has to say, why they ran away, I think you'll change your mind. So if you won't sit down, I'll tell you standing up. Annabelle hit her, first with a broom and then with a poker, and did something with the dog . . ."

Jack looked as if he feared he was losing his mind. "Dog? What dog? We don't have a dog, we've never had a dog. What the devil are you talking about?"

At the same time, Annabelle spoke rapidly and with great intensity. "Laurie's a liar, you know that, she always has been. Just like her father, he lied about everything, even when there was no reason for it . . ."

"Look at Laurie, Jack. Look at her face and her arms. Where do you think she got the bruises?

They're fresh ones, still forming, even."

Nell reached down and unbuttoned Laurie's shirt, and pushed it off her shoulder to show a rising and discolored welt. "That was done just before the kids left home. So was that mark on Tim's face. With a poker, Jack. And here, there's a lump here behind Laurie's ear that she got when her mother actually knocked her out. Unconscious, Jack. Tim thought she'd been killed. Do you approve of your wife disciplining children with an iron poker?"

"She's lying!" Annabelle cried. "She'll do anything to get attention, Laurie will, even to—"

"Even to hitting herself with a poker?" Nell asked, still quietly. "No. She couldn't have hit herself that way if she'd tried. And it isn't just Laurie's word for it; Tim was there. Tim tried to stop her from beating Laurie, and Annabelle struck him, too. Do you think Tim would lie about a thing like that? Do you think if they were running away simply because they'd been naughty and been punished in an ordinary way, they'd have come running to me? Do you?"

Jack put a hand on the back of a chair, as if he needed something to lean on. The color had washed out of his face, and he was listening now. "Annabelle? What's she talking about?"

"She hurt us, and then she hurt the puppy, too," Tim said. He'd been trying to speak for several minutes. "Ask her what she did to him! Ask her where's Amigo?"

Annabelle faced her husband, speaking to him alone. "You know I'm terrified of dogs! I told you how one bit me when I was a child, and I've been terrified of them ever since! They'd been hiding a dog out in the ravine, and when they brought it into the house I insisted they get rid of it, and it came at me and bit me . . . and they were insolent, and I hit Laurie because she had no right to speak to me the way she did, and . . ."

Jack was staring at her with something like horror growing in his eyes. "With a *poker*? You hit the kid with a *poker*?"

Annabelle's face was wild, wilder than anyone had ever seen her, . . . except Laurie. Laurie had seen her this way often enough. As always, it made her tremble, but Nell's hand was still on her shoulder warm and strong. Laurie unconsciously leaned a little closer to the older woman.

"I don't know," Annabelle said. "I picked up something, but don't you understand, the dog bit me, and I was *wild* with fear, and I hit her with something . . . but she's not seriously hurt, you can see that . . ."

"What did you do with Amigo?" Tim demanded again, growing braver as his father seemed to be backing off, his grandmother holding her own on their behalf.

"Annabelle." Jack sounded as if he were having trouble breathing. "What did you do to the dog?"

"I got rid of it! They had no right to have it, and

they brought it in the house and it bit me and I was *afraid* of it, so I got rid of it! It's gone; you'll never see it again!"

"And you beat Laurie with a poker, a little kid like that," Jack said, sounding sick.

"And that's only the beginning," Nell said. "Or maybe I've got it the wrong way around, because I hope it's the last thing she'll do to Laurie. Only you haven't heard half of what she's already done. You always thought Laurie was sort of a funny kid. Well, it amazes me that she isn't odder than she is, considering the way her mother's been abusing her for years."

"That's not true! I have not abused her, she's a liar, a compulsive liar," Annabelle protested. "Anybody who ever knew her will tell you what a liar Laurie is!"

"Like who?" Nell asked. For a moment the room was silent, while for once it was Annabelle who tried to think of something to say. "I don't know who Annabelle can find to testify to Laurie being a liar, but I think there are a number of people who'll testify to the abuse. Maybe they didn't know Annabelle was the one who did it, but I think they'll tell you a few interesting things, Jack. Like how she was always going to school with different kinds of injuries. Burns, broken bones, cuts that had to be sewed up . . ."

"She's clumsy!" Annabelle cried in great agitation. "She has accidents all the time, she falls and cuts herself and—"

Nell went right on speaking. "Talk to the people at the hospitals where Annabelle took the child to have her fixed up. Find out how many times they moved because someone at a hospital began to get suspicious. Talk to the teachers where she went to school and see how often Laurie turned up with injuries. See how many injuries there were. And then see how many people ever remember seeing Laurie be clumsy, fall and hurt herself, burn herself, cut herself . . . *who besides Annabelle ever saw her do any of those things?*"

And Jack, too, believed.

Laurie was watching his face, and she read it there as clearly as if it were printed in red letters.

Jack believed.

He looked sick, as sick as Laurie herself had often felt.

And Annabelle read it, too. She flung herself upon her husband, crying, still protesting her innocence, proclaiming Laurie's guilt, even though she must have known it was too late for that.

"Your wife is a sick woman, Jack," Nell said, and then she turned away, looking so tired, so tired. She paused. "I think the kids had better stay here with me until you've taken Annabelle to a doctor or somebody, until you know what you want to do about her."

Laurie heard these words in a sort of wonder that made her eyes brim with tears.

She didn't have to go home with Annabelle. After all these years, someone was going to help her.

TEN

LAURIE WOKE SOBBING AND reached for the light beside her bed, only to encounter nothing but a bare wooden surface where the lamp should have been.

She felt frightened, and then gradually she remembered. She wasn't at home; she was in Nell's little house, in one of the twin beds in the guest room, with Shelly asleep in the other one.

She sat for a moment on the edge of the bed until she realized she'd been having a nightmare and could stop crying. She needed a handkerchief, and she didn't have one. Wasn't there a box of tissues in the bathroom?

But before she could stand up and try to make her way there in the unfamiliar darkness, the overhead light was switched on and Nell stood in the doorway. She was wearing an old cotton nightgown, and she looked concerned.

"Laurie? Are you all right?"

Laurie nodded her head. "I was having a bad dream." She accepted the hanky Nell handed over to her and wiped at her nose. "I thought...she was beating Amigo, and even after he was all bloody and...and dead...she kept on hitting him with the poker."

"Dreams can be pretty bad, sometimes," Nell agreed. "And after the day you had yesterday, it's no wonder you're having nightmares. Do you think you can go back to sleep now, or would you like to talk for a while?"

"I'm all right, I think. Now I know it's only a dream," Laurie said, but even as she said it, she was troubled. What *had* Annabelle done with Amigo? There hadn't been any blood on the kitchen floor when she came to, but it wouldn't have taken much of a blow to kill a little dog like Amigo.

"Well, good night again, then," Nell said, and turned out the light. Laurie heard her padding back across the hall to her own bedroom; she didn't close the door, and Laurie felt a surge of gratitude. Nell had come to comfort her, and now she was leaving the doors open between them so that if Laurie had any more bad dreams, Nell would hear her.

It was some time before she went back to sleep. She kept thinking about Annabelle, and what Nell had said about her being sick, and how Jack was going to take her to a doctor, maybe even already had, because she was hysterical and wouldn't stop crying and telling everyone that it wasn't true she'd mistreated her daughter. She'd just kept on insisting that Laurie was awkward and clumsy and she was always hurting herself.

And then she must have fallen asleep, because the next thing she knew it was morning. There were birds singing outside the window and sunshine sifting through the curtains, and she could smell coffee and toast from the kitchen.

She had to dress in the same jeans and shirt she'd taken off the night before, and they weren't very clean. She put them on, her fingers fumbling over the buttons in her nervousness.

How long would they be able to stay here with Nell? What if the doctor believed Annabelle and said there was nothing wrong with her? If she was sick, it was in her mind, wasn't it, not in her body? So how would the doctor know what was in her mind? Would he say there was nothing wrong with her, so then she'd go home and insist that Laurie come home, too?

No, she couldn't go back to Annabelle. They mustn't make her do that. Surely Nell would be able to keep them from making her do that, because Nell believed Laurie had told the truth.

Everyone else was already up. They were having cocoa with marshmallows in the bright little kitchen, and Nell was ladling out bowls of hot cereal.

Surprisingly, Laurie was hungry, and she ate everything Nell put before her. Just as they were finishing up, there was a telephone call. And to her surprise, it was for Laurie.

She almost never had calls, and no one knew she was at Nell's house except Jack and Annabelle. Laurie took the telephone with an uneasy feeling that eased when she recognized Mrs. Gerrold's voice.

"Laurie? I talked to your father, I mean your stepfather, this morning, and he told me where you were. He said your mother is ill and that you kids were going to stay with his mother for a few days; and when I told George that, he got very upset and wanted to know about Amigo. He was so agitated I insisted he tell me what it was all about, so I know you had a puppy down there in the woods. Can I tell George that the dog's all right, that you're still taking care of him? Or is there something I should be doing about him?"

The breakfast that had, only moments before, made a comforting warmth in her stomach now seemed heavy and distressing. Laurie swallowed hard and blinked against the tears. "I . . . we don't know where Amigo is, Mrs. Gerrold. My . . . my mother said she . . . got rid of him."

There was a small silence, and then Mrs. Gerrold let out a sigh. "Oh, Laurie! I'm so sorry. And

George is going to be.... Well, you couldn't help that, whatever it was that happened. I suppose I'll have to tell him when I go back this evening. Or maybe you'd want to talk to him yourself? I can give you the telephone number of the hospital, if you want to call him, he's in room 417."

How could she tell him? When she was so upset about it herself! Wouldn't it be bad for him? She struggled to say something, but before she could get anything out, Mrs. Gerrold said, "No, of course you don't want to be the one to break the bad news. I'll tell him myself. But maybe in a few days, when you have time, you'd like to call George? He's so lonesome, and I know he misses you. In about a week he'll be able to have visitors. Maybe you could go see him sometimes. I'd be happy to pick you up if it's all right with your grandmother."

Laurie wrote down the number at the hospital, and George's room number, but she dreaded talking to him about what had happened to Amigo, even if his mother had already broken the bad news.

When she hung up the phone, Nell was stacking dishes in the sink, and she turned to look at Laurie. "If you can do the washing up, I think I'll go over to Jack's and get you kids some clothes and maybe talk to him, see what they're going to do. If I don't get back by noon, just make yourselves some sandwiches. There are cookies in the cookie jar and plenty of milk."

So Laurie washed the dishes, and Tim dried them,

and then together they made the beds and tidied up the house. It was a nice house, but it was small, Laurie thought. Tim had slept on the couch in the living room last night, while she and Shelly had shared the one extra bedroom. Surely Nell wouldn't try to keep all of them there for long, when she didn't even have sleeping space for them. And if she could only keep two, it would be her own grand-children, naturally.

When everything was in order, Tim and Shelly went out in the backyard to play. Laurie didn't feel like playing. She picked up a magazine and tried to read it, but she didn't feel like reading, either. She kept listening for Nell's car and hoping that what-ever the news was, it wouldn't mean she'd have to go back to Annabelle.

When she finally heard a car in the driveway, Laurie rushed to the door, but it wasn't Nell. It was Jack.

He came slowly up the steps and across the porch, pulling open the screen. He looked as if he hadn't been to bed; he was wearing the same clothes he'd had on last night and he needed a shave. She'd never seen him look so exhausted.

"Hi, Laurie. Where is everybody?" he asked in a tired voice.

She told him, and he nodded. "I don't suppose Ma left the coffeepot on, did she?"

Nell had, and Laurie got him a cup of coffee and stood awkwardly beside the kitchen table when

Jack sat down to drink it. His shoulders sagged, and there was nothing booming about his voice now.

"Sit down, Laurie. I'm going to have to talk to you," Jack said. Here it comes, Laurie thought, as she slid into the chair opposite him. But what was it going to be?

He took a drink of coffee and then held the cup between both of his big hands, as though they were cold and he was warming them on the mug. He had a little trouble getting started, as if, like Laurie, he found it difficult to know what to say. He kept stopping to clear his throat and once he paused to blow his nose.

"I took Annabelle to the hospital last night. She was so upset she couldn't stop crying and talking. She was still denying, right up to a few minutes ago, that she'd mistreated you."

Laurie said nothing, but she felt her heart begin to pound in her chest. He couldn't believe Annabelle instead of her, could he? Not when he'd heard what Tim had to say, too.

"She's sick, Laurie," Jack said. "I don't know how she could be so sick and I didn't notice anything. But I suppose it was because I was gone so much, and she was on her good behavior when I was home. The doctor talked to her for a long time this morning, about her own childhood. And about her marriage to your father. I guess you know she's very bitter about your father, about the way he deserted her."

Laurie nodded, and it was a little easier for her to breathe, now, though she was still wary.

"I guess she's taken it out on you, because all the people she's depended on in her life have disappointed her. She couldn't hit back at your father, because he went away, so she took it out on you. But the doctor thinks that isn't the main reason she's been . . . the reason she's hurt you."

Jack took another deep breath and then another swallow of coffee, as if talking this way were very painful to him. "The doctor said maybe what she does doesn't have anything to do with you, at all.

"You see, many parents who mistreat their kids do it because they, themselves, were mistreated by their parents, years before. And it makes a sort of sickness in them that they can't control. It doesn't mean that she hates you, or that she doesn't care what happens to you. It just means she's unhappy and she can't help it, the things she does."

He ran a hand over his chin and she heard the rasp of whiskers. "You know she always saw to it that you had the right food and decent clothes, and she bought presents she thought you'd like. I guess some of the times when she's hurt *you* have been when she was angry or upset with *me*, when I let her down by not getting home when we had special plans or something, when she was disappointed, especially if she was having a headache at the same time, well, she'd hit out at you."

He drew in a long breath, as if that speech had

taken almost everything out of him. She'd never thought about grown-ups having trouble knowing what to say, but she couldn't doubt that Jack was struggling with this. "I didn't know it was going on, Laurie," he said now. "I'm . . . I'm sorry."

Laurie sat on the edge of the chair, scarcely able to breathe, saying nothing. This man was quite different from the Jack she had known, the big, bluff, cheerful man with the booming voice who thought she was an "odd kid."

Jack sat twisting the coffee cup around and around in his hands. "Annabelle is going to have to stay in the hospital for a few days. They're going to talk to her a lot and ask her more questions. Probably they'll let her come home by the end of the week, though."

Laurie stopped breathing altogether, waiting for the worst.

"The doctor wouldn't say for sure, until he's made his final evaluation at the end of the week, but he thinks she'll be able to come home. Only she'll have to go back and see him about twice a week for a long time, and he thinks it would be better if none of you kids were there for a while."

Something rigid relaxed a little inside Laurie.

"Ma said she'd keep all of you, at least for the summer. It's a small house, but you'll all spend a lot of time outdoors. We'll get a cot and put it up on the back porch for Tim; it's screened, so it will serve as a bedroom as long as it's warm. I hope you don't mind, staying here with Ma. I don't know where to find any of your own relatives, and it upsets Annabelle if I try to talk to her about it."

"I won't mind," Laurie said softly, and the entire summer opened up before her, free and golden. Only the loss of George and Amigo cast a shadow over it.

"Eventually," Jack was going on, "I hope we can all get together as a family again. I love your mother, Laurie. Maybe that's hard for you to understand, considering how she's treated you. I think she's very unhappy about doing the things she did. She needs a lot of help now to learn how to handle her problems without taking them out on you. The doctor thinks she can be helped. And when she's better, we'll all live together again. But until then, I think we're going to keep you separated, you kids and Annabelle."

He cleared his throat again and poured more coffee, and he was so uncomfortable that Laurie started to feel uncomfortable with him, waiting for whatever was going to come next.

"Her own mother mistreated her very badly, Laurie, and somehow that's why she's the way she is. She told the doctor some really terrible things that happened to her as a child, things she's never told anyone before. It's helped her some, already, to be able to tell the doctor about them. And maybe, when she gets that all out of her system, she won't have to hurt you anymore. Until we're sure that's the case, you'll be safe here with Ma."

Laurie stared at him across the table, her tongue snaking across her lips before she could speak in a husky voice. "I . . . wouldn't ever hurt my kids, just because my mother hurt me."

Jack's mouth softened in a tired smile. "I know you wouldn't, Laurie. We're going to help your mother, and you're going to know what it's all about, what caused it. And when you have children of your own some day, you won't need to take anything out on them because you'll know better." He lifted his head to listen. "Is that Ma coming home now?"

It was. They heard Tim and Shelly shouting with excitement, and when Nell came in, Laurie saw the reason why and nearly shouted herself.

For Nell carried in her arms a squirming mass of silky golden fur; Amigo licked at every hand and face that came within his range, and Laurie was unable to control the tears that mingled with her laughter when the dog was put into her lap.

"Boy, what a character!" Nell said, laughing. "I thought he'd lick me to pieces on the way home!"

Tim asked the question that Laurie couldn't, because of the lump in her throat.

"Where did you find him?"

"At the pound. It took me a while to figure out what Annabelle would logically have done with him. If she was afraid of him . . . and she was . . . the easiest way to dispose of an animal is to call the

164

pound and have them pick him up. So I asked if they'd let me look at any puppies they'd picked up yesterday, and there he was. They even had her name and address where they got him, so I knew it was Amigo."

Laurie nodded, smiling through her tears.

"This place isn't going to be the same with three kids and a dog around," Jack said, smiling faintly. "You sure you can stand it, Ma?"

"I'll make it through the summer," Nell promised. "I've got a garden, I'll put the kids to work in it; and we'll fence off a corner for Amigo, so he doesn't dig up anything we don't want dug. When it's time for school to start, well, we'll just have to wait and see."

Wait and see, Laurie thought. No guarantees of what would happen. She'd probably have to go back and live with Annabelle in September. But maybe, if Jack was right, Annabelle would be different by then.

And if she wasn't . . . well, Laurie thought, she'd be able to talk to either Jack or Nell. And know that they would listen to her, know that they would believe her.

"You know what I think?" Nell asked as she poured herself a cup of coffee. "I think Tim could unload the suitcases from the back of the car. And I think Laurie ought to make a telephone call."

Looking up as she squeezed a struggling Amigo against her chest, Laurie said, "A telephone call?"

"Yes. To that boy, George, at the hospital. Before his mother tells him Amigo's been lost, you can tell him the dog's been found. And one of these days, when George can have visitors, we'll all go and see him. He sounds like quite a brave boy to me."

"You're pretty brave yourself, Ma," Jack said, "taking on this menagerie."

"Oh, we'll manage," Nell said, and she smiled.

But Laurie scarcely saw or heard them. She handed Amigo over to Tim, dialed the number, and in a minute George's voice came on the line.

"George?" she said, "Listen, George, you're never going to believe what an adventure Amigo has had . . ."

And all the time she talked to him, deep inside her a spring was unwinding, a spring that had been a tight, painful part of her for a long time, and in its place a seed had been planted. A seed of joy that would grow and grow.